TEARS OF ABANDON

OLIVER PHIPPS

Gray Door Ltd.

ISBN 978—0-9896012-6-9

TABLE OF CONTENTS

Oliver Phipps

CHAPTER ONE: A DARING PLAN

Their faces appeared stern, as if weathered by a sheer force of purpose. The shovels, picks, and other articles of life that could be seen around them presented an apparent effort for daily survival. Drew examined the fellows in the old black and white photos with a discerning interest he hadn't done before. He studied their grizzled beards; their coarse clothing, and the harsh woodland that hovered all around. Somehow, these men had taken on nature and held the wilderness at bay with crude tools of a bygone day and will power alone.

Drew tried to visualize himself in the picture. Perhaps somewhere in the background, standing with a pick in hand, maybe by the large sluice box; or kneeling by the stream with a gold pan, having just picked up a container full of Gods' essential element. He tried to imagine himself hiking up the forest covered hills with a backpack and a walking staff. But he just couldn't see himself enduring such hardships for very long, no matter how hard he tried. He knew he didn't have a physical stature built for an extended stay in the rugged environment of Alaska and he wouldn't attempt to deceive himself into thinking such a thing.

He closed the large book and laid it back on the coffee table in front of him. Picking up his drink he scanned the front again. The title indicated something to do with the Alaskan Gold rush in pictures.

He gazed across the coffee table at his roommate Richard, who he's called Rich for as long as he can remember. Rich had the rugged features of an outdoorsman; the unruly locks of brown hair and square jaw. He could picture Rich in Alaska, by a stream with a gold pan in hand.

He and Rich had been best friends through high school and entered college together. Rich had always been the more outgoing of the two.

While they both suited up for the high school football team, Rich played and Drew warmed the bench. Drew admired his friend's physical prowess. Drew just always seemed to be the semi-nerd, or brains of the duo. While Rich inclined more towards the muscles persona in their friendship.

The sound of rock music crept back to his senses and the several drinks he had already drunk began to take full effect; he looked at Jack as he leaned on the armrest talking to Rich. Jack certainly fit his image of a confident and well to do guy. Drew had come to regard that confidence as a thinly disguised arrogance, however.

Jack came from a wealthy family and there would be no doubt he would stroll into a CEO position somewhere after graduation. The cushy life Jack had laid before him didn't bother Drew so much as the position he'd taken between himself and Rich over the last few years. Jack and Rich both retained a zeal for adventure. Jack took a shine to Rich in their first year of college and since that time he'd become a wedge, slowly splitting Drew and his best friend apart.

Although he, Rich, Jack and Cindy; Jack's girlfriend, were all in their early twenties, there had always seemed to be a separation and hierarchy between them due to financial standing. Drew casually scanned Jack's apartment and found no difficulty noticing the difference. The living room of Jack's apartment would hold the entire apartment he and Rich shared. Rich had become very fond of Jack and Cindy's little drinking and socializing parties, but Drew had begun to enjoy them less and less.

"So Drew, you in or not?" Jack turned to Drew as his conversation with Rich found a stopping point.

"Yeah Drew, what's it going to be, you in?" Rich sounded like someone who'd been put off as long as he cared to be.

"Well, you know guys; Alaska seems to be a pretty dangerous place if you ask me." Drew cringed a little inside as this came out more sheepishly than he'd intended.

"Ohhh," Jack wailed in the condescending tone Drew had become accustom to. "You hear that Cindy." Jack turned and spoke in a voice loud enough to carry over the music. "Alaska is a dangerous place!" Cindy sat at the bar directly behind Rich watching a show on TV.

"What are you saying about me? You know I'm trying to watch this show Jack."

Jack now began to show his level of intoxication. Drew felt the only reason to get Cindy involved would be to make Drew appear weak.

Cindy and Jack had become a couple the first year of school and Jack had encouraged her to find someone for Rich in an apparent attempt to corner Rich's friendship. Though she found several available girls over the course of their schooling, Rich didn't seem able to hold onto one.

But, since Drew never actually had a real girlfriend before, he often found himself in a position of the third wheel. Even his prom date was more of a mutual agreement than an actual date. The so called "date" was a girl who didn't function well with the opposite sex either.

Regardless of this, he refused to let Jack take over his friendship with Rich. On the other hand, Rich seemed oblivious to what Drew perceived as a straightforward attempt by Jack to push him out of the picture.

Jack turned back to Drew and continued. "You know Drew, this is 1992 not 1892. Things have changed since the gold rush days in those pictures. I hear Alaska has electricity and even running water now."

Drew now pushed his glasses back up on his nose in what had become something of a nervous habit.

"Come on Drew it'll be fun, you can hang out with Cindy if you like," Jack now spoke with a stifled laugh.

"Hey, I heard my name again. What are you setting me up for," Cindy said with some frustration as she glanced at them from behind the bar.

"I know Drew, you can ask that new girl to come along," Rich jumped into the conversation with an increasingly rare intercession.

"New girl," exclaimed Jack, appearing very much in the mood to belittle Drew in a manner thinly disguised as buddy jokes. "I don't recall there ever being any old girls; much less a new one Rich?" Jack smirked again as he then finished his drink.

"You remember that girl Ashley he dated for a while Jack?"

Drew recalled the friend he used to know as Rich made an obvious attempt to keep some of the heat off of him. But he felt Jack would take every advantage at this point.

"Actually Rich, I only went out with Ashley one time." Drew again felt his reply sounded weak.

"There you go then, once is enough for me, so this girl is the new girl then,"

quiet surprisingly Jack took an about face.

Regardless of this, Drew didn't want to bring Beth into the conversation; particularly a somewhat alcohol infused one. He and Beth met in the college library a few weeks before the semester ended. Due to what he considered the somewhat rough nature of his friends, he intentionally kept their dates a secret.

After two months of this quiet relationship with Beth, Rich discovered Drew was dating a girl. So, with the secret out, Drew had invited her to come by the apartment sometime so she could meet his friends.

"Well, maybe I can mention the trip to her when I see her again."
He hoped this might move the subject away from Beth.

"Yeah Drew, and tell this 'new girl' the trip is all expenses paid, so
she needn't worry

about spending school money or money for those girlie things she
may need." Drew gazed across the coffee table at Jack and wondered
if he could actually be making an attempt to be nice or simply
implying the only girls Drew could date would be the ones with little
money.

"Sure, yes I'll tell her Jack. Thanks again for the offer. I'm getting a
bit tired so if you'll excuse me, I believe I'll head back to the
apartment."

"Yeah all right, just go ahead and leave when things are picking
up," Jack snickered again indicating he'd not finished with Drew yet
and wished to get one more snide remark in.

On the way back to the apartment he and Rich shared, Drew smiled
slightly as he thought about Beth. She had that girl next door beauty,
with brown hair that flowed around in a free sort of way. She stood
about five foot five inches and seemed to prefer wearing shoes that
would help her stand a few inches taller. She always glowed with
enthusiasm and he couldn't remember a time that she'd been upset
about anything. He recalled how nervous he became before asking her
out on a date the day they met.

Then he chuckled a little when he thought of what he told her. On
their third date he brought up that she sometimes had a 'sad smile.' She
giggled and told him there wasn't such a thing. Only Beth could get
her cute little mouth to make a pouty twist that way. Drew couldn't
think of any other way to describe the unique expression. This seemed
to be a special Beth characteristic and he loved that about her.

The next morning Drew crawled out of bed, prepared for a usual Saturday morning. After a routine visit to the bathroom he went to the small area they called the kitchen.

Rich had come in sometime during the night but Drew had no idea when. After a light breakfast he sat down to watch some TV. No sooner had he switched the television on the phone rang.

"Hello?"

"Hi Drew! How are you?" He knew the voice and immediately his demeanor improved upon hearing Beth on the other end.

"Well, I'm doing all right. I was just, ah, watching some cartoons." He wanted to be a little more humorous; Rich told him girls wanted their guys to make them laugh occasionally. Beth did laugh at the cartoon answer and Drew smiled. He even surprised himself at being able to make a witty comment that early in the morning.

"Do you think I could come by and see you today?"

Drew scanned the apartment trying to estimate how much time he needed to get the place half way clean.

"Sure, that would be great Beth. I thought about you last night and how I'd enjoy seeing you sometime this weekend."

"Yeah, I thought the same thing," she replied happily. "How about forty-five minutes or so, would that be all right?"

"Yeah, that would be great," he immediately began picking up some dirty laundry from the floor. "Do you want me to meet you somewhere to make sure you get here all right?"

"Nah, that's okay, I'm sure I know where the apartment is. Could you give me the number again though, just to make sure I remember it right?"

"211."

"All right, that's what I thought. I'll see you soon, bye."

"Okay, see you soon then, bye."

What might be called a cleaning tornado ensued immediately after Drew hung up. He hid dirty dishes, crammed dirty clothes in the closet, and tried to camouflage stains on the end table. He jumped in the shower, dropped the soap several times, and spilled half the bottle of shampoo in an attempt to finish in three minutes.

Glancing at the clock as he dressed and brushed his hair Drew felt confident he would be ready in time, but the chime of the door bell dispelled this notion. With no socks or shoes on Drew strolled through the living room scanning around to be sure the small apartment would be presentable. Opening the door, sunshine streamed in around the wide smile and shapely silhouette of Beth.

"Hi, I hope you didn't have plans or anything, I just thought if you weren't busy..."

"No, no I had a lazy day planned. I'm glad you called," Drew opened the door to let her in. He noticed Beth cradled a book close to her chest as she might a purse or something valuable.

"Please have a seat anywhere."

Beth sat down and Drew took a seat across from her. "I'm really glad you came to visit Beth."

"I'm umm, glad you're glad I came to visit," she said with a little giggle. "Do I need to take my shoes off?"

This puzzled Drew and he glanced down at her feet. She had a nice pair of sandals on and her toenails were painted a crimson red.

"I don't know. Do you want to take your shoes off?" as the awkwardness between the two became more apparent.

"Well, I just thought maybe because of the carpet or something," she then nodded at his feet. Drew looked down and realized in the rush he'd forgotten to put socks or shoes on.

"Oh, no, I see what you mean; no I just wanted to let you in and forgot I'd not put my socks or shoes on." They both laughed which seemed to relieve some of the awkward tension.

"What do you have there?" Drew pointed to the book.

"Oh, this is Candace Clarendon's' new mystery 'River Boat.' I just love her mysteries. I've always got one of her books with me. In fact, there have been times that one of her books has been the only thing to keep me from being alone." Beth giggled a little as if she'd told a secret. "Have you read any of her books?"

"Umm," Drew struggled to recall any of her books he'd ever read. "I did read some of her book 'Desert Flower.'" This had some truth to it as he'd picked the book up in a store once and flipped through the pages reading bits and pieces.

"I love that one," Beth seemed to get excited now, sitting up straighter as if ready to get into a deep discussion on the matter. "I would love to be able to write the way Candace does." She now took a very serious tone. Drew realized this must be important to her and in an effort to avoid talking in-depth about "Desert Flower" yet remain on subject; he took the opportunity to encourage her.

"You could do that, I'm sure you could."

"What, you really think I could write like Candace Clarendon? Oh you are a sweetheart Drew, but let's be for real."

"Well, I believe you could write like her someday, I mean you can do anything you want. You should let me help you Beth." Drew struggled a bit due to his experience, or lack thereof, with girls. Still he felt he had at least been staying afloat.

"You're really too good to be true Drew, you know that."

"I am serious Beth," Drew wanted to make sure she understood him. He looked her straight in the eyes. "I promise you Beth, I'll be there for you no matter what. You tell me you want my help and neither heaven or hell will keep me from being there for you."

Beth gazed shyly back into his eyes and realized he meant what he'd just said. She moved out of her seat and quickly ascended upon Drew to give him a quick kiss on the cheek as she giggled a little and just as quickly sat back in her chair.

Drew was surprised and happy to get this little peck on the cheek as Beth had always been very conservative with her affections towards him. Even after many dates, she had yet to give Drew a kiss on the lips; though he made several attempts and she always reacted as if she wasn't ready yet. He finally decided he wouldn't move too fast for her and mess anything up. He cared too much about her already to do anything that might derail this relationship.

In the hall behind Drew a door opened. This caused Beth to look behind him. Then her eyes opened wide, she let out a little scream and immediately dropped the book to her lap and put her hands up in an effort to cover her eyes. Turning around, Drew saw Rich standing in the doorway with his boxer shorts on and nothing else.

"Oh man, I'm sorry; I didn't know you had company Drew." Rich spoke as if still half asleep.

Drew had completely forgotten about Rich during his campaign to present an acceptable atmosphere for Beth. Yet here Rich stood; with his hair sticking up, a five o'clock shadow and checkered boxer shorts. The sudden appearance of Rich seemed to totally derail his efforts of appearing civilized to Beth. Rich backed out of the doorway and to his room.

"I'm so sorry, that's the roommate I was telling you about." Beth opened her fingers slightly on her right hand exposing her eye.

"Can I lower my hands now?" The words came through her covered face somewhat muffled.

"Yeah, you're as safe as you'll ever be with Rich around." They both laughed.

10

Rich strolled through the doorway again but this time with sweat pants and a T-shirt on. He raked his hair over with his fingers and then bounced over the couch to land beside Drew. "So Buddy, who's your friend here, she's a real cutie." Rich winked at Beth and her face grimaced just a little, as if to deflect his advance gently.

"Elizabeth Reynolds this is Richard Harrison. My friend since grade school and current roommate," he said waving a hand from Beth to Rich.

"Please call me Rich."

"And you can call me Beth," she said as they shook hands.

"Well, I'm glad to finally meet you Beth. I think you have Drew here stuck on you."

"Come on Rich!" Drew protested, though this was actually something he wanted her to know.

"Really Rich, you don't say!" Beth looked at Drew as if a little suspicious of him and then laughed a bit to ease the tension.

"So Beth, you two going or not? We will be leaving next week with or without you two."

"Going?" She turned to Drew with a puzzled expression and then back to Rich as she shrugged her shoulders. Drew had decided not to mention the trip until a more private setting but again Rich interrupted that plan.

Looking puzzled as he turned directly to Rich, "You mean to tell me you still haven't said anything to her about it?"

"I planned too Rich, but she's only been here a few minutes. And I wish you would have let me bring it up," as he quickly looked at Beth trying to gage her reaction to the information Rich had just blurted out.

"Bring what up? Would someone let me in on the secret?" Beth appeared to not be amused in the least.

"Alaska," Rich blurted out before Drew could say anything. "Do you want to go to Alaska with us? Drew should have asked you already."

"Alaska?" She was perplexed by the whole situation. "What's he talking about Drew?"

"Well, Jack, a friend of ours and his girlfriend Cindy are planning a trip to Alaska. The plan pretty much amounts to the five of us kayaking down one of the rivers; camping and all that outdoors type stuff."

Rich, now seeming content that Drew had spoken to Beth about the plan, bounced off the couch and into the kitchen area directly adjacent to the small living room.

"Hey Drew… did you wash the dishes? Wait, where are the dishes? Drew, did you put the dirty dishes in the oven?" Rolling his eyes and grimacing to the fact Rich now seemed on a mission to sabotage everything; Drew simply decided not to acknowledge his friend.

Beth however, smiled slyly at Drew as if she had just learned something about him she would've never expected. Drew smiled, seeming embarrassed, and shrugged his shoulders indicating he'd been caught.

"Alaska, wow," she said getting back to the conversation at hand. "That all sounds great. But I can't go. I can't possibly afford a trip to Alaska."

"All expenses paid," Rich shouted while his head remained almost entirely inside the refrigerator, but apparently still able to keep up with the conversation. "Hey Drew didn't we have some mustard?"

"Rich, would you let me handle this please, and yes we have some mustard. Wait, what are you eating in the morning that you need mustard for?" forgetting for a brief moment Beth was still sitting across from him.

12

"All expenses paid? Really Drew?" Beth stared at him as if awaiting a confirmation. Rich meanwhile jumped over the back of the couch in another display of his athletic prowess. This time he had a hot dog in one hand and a can of soda in the other.

"Yeah our friend Jack is paying for it. He's loaded! Tell her Drew," Rich motioned with his elbow since both hands were full.

"Why do I need to tell her anything Rich, you're doing a fine job. And really, hot-dogs for breakfast?"

"Yeah, it's the breakfast of great athletes everywhere," came a muffled reply from a mouth half full of hot dog.

"So how long is this trip going to be for?" She asked. Rich, still eating, started to speak but Drew turned to him with an obviously irritated stare.

"Oh, please go ahead buddy. I'm just trying to help."

Drew turned back to Beth and replied. "It'll only be a few weeks. The weather will start turning bad up in Alaska if we don't go soon. We went to Colorado last year and Wyoming the year before.

Rich had to make up some classes this summer so we didn't think there would be a trip. Then Jack came up with the idea of kayaking down an Alaskan river and as he put it 'exchange a quality trip for quantity trip.'

"Before you make a decision Beth I think you should know this won't be a pleasure cruise. I don't know how you feel about camping, but we'll be sleeping on the ground in small tents and eating packaged meals." Beth thought for a moment, and both guys stared at her in anticipation.

"I think I could handle that," she said after a moment of thought.

"All right then," Rich blurted out. "It's all settled; we are going to Alaska! I'll go tell Jack so we can get the tickets and everything set up." Rich bounced into his room, and a "whoopee" sounded out behind the closed door.

"Beth, you may want to think this over a bit more. Don't let Rich rush you into anything." Drew spoke with a face of concern.

"Well, I think if I'm ever going to write as well as Candace Clarendon I've got to get out in the world and do something. There's no way I could afford to go to Alaska and for me, this seems to be an opportunity I won't often get, if ever again."

Just then Rich came through the door and grabbing his car keys from a change dish in the bookshelf; he went out the door with a quick "see you guys later."

"Yes, I understand that," Drew said getting back to the conversation. "But I think you'll find Jack to be way over confident. He also drinks too much. When we went to Colorado last year, I know of several occasions which flat out frightened me due to his arrogant and somewhat alcohol-induced behavior."

Beth thought about this for a moment. Then she looked at Drew.

"I understand your concern, but as long as you're there, I'll be safe. Surely your competent thoughts can keep things balanced out, right?"

Drew smiled a little. He felt good that Beth thought such a thing about him. He then continued.

"Well, maybe, but other things besides Jack's drinking and over confidence may affect the trip. For example, I've known Rich most of my life, and we've always been great friends. After becoming friends with Jack though he's changed. He doesn't have the money Jack has, but he's beginning to act the way Jack acts. He wants the things Jack has, but I just don't think he'll ever be as successful as Jack. One reason being his family isn't as wealthy as Jack's."

"And did I mention Cindy? Cindy is like Jack in being over confident to the point of arrogance. She also has something of a superiority complex in my opinion. She seems to gravitate towards

14

money and power. Although she's athletic and knows her way around a campsite, she doesn't do any more of the work than necessary.

The gist of it is, you may not be treated as well as you should by her. And I'm suspect of Jack and Rich's abilities with a trip of this scale."

Beth reclined back in her chair as a sail falling when the wind suddenly dies. "So, you think we shouldn't go?" she asked after some thought.

"It's not that I'm saying we shouldn't go. Possibly more along the line of, I don't want you to expect a relaxing vacation. Then the trip turns out to be an exercise of putting up with three somewhat eccentric characters for two weeks. Cindy will most likely not be your best friend and possibly not any friend at all.

Jack thrives on taking things to far in an effort for him appear as some a hero. And Rich has more or less become a student of Jack. Basically, if we go, we should probably go without any unrealistic expectations. If you're all right with that, then I say we should go. But if you're expecting a leisure trip we may need to reconsider."

Beth now appeared to consider what Drew said. Then after a few moments, she seemed to have made a decision.

"I would like to go. I understand your concern, and I respect that you want me to be clear about the trip, but I don't think I'm as fragile as people may think. I'm really frightened I'll be upset with myself later if I pass the opportunity simply because of possible challenges."

Drew didn't get surprised at the decision. He suspected she would want to go but wanted to be sure she understood the circumstances.

"All right then, we'll go." He relaxed a bit now that she understood what they might be in for and a decision had been made.

"I suppose I should get ready then." Beth said with some excitement.

Yeah, that is probably a good idea." Drew said. "I'll let you know when we'll be leaving, as soon as I hear from Jack or Rich. I'll also make sure to reserve us a nice roomy tent if possible." Drew smiled with the best suave, male type smile he could muster.

"Hey now, don't get any ideas," Beth moved back a bit into her chair, "you know I'm not that type of girl Drew." She had a very firm voice but smiled a little. Drew immediately tried to fix any possible damage.

"Oh yeah, I know that Beth, separate tents, I was just kidding around."

"I'll call you Monday to check in," she said rising from her chair, leaning over giving Drew another little peck on the cheek before she walked to the door, opened it and left quietly. The kiss didn't exactly meet his hoped for expectations, but after the intense experience with Rich, he considered this another small step in the right direction.

CHAPTER TWO: WHISPER

The following week everything had been set up for the trip. Beth called Drew several times throughout the week and he would relay the plan. Thursday morning she arrived at his door, smiling as usual and prepared to fly out that afternoon.

"Is that all the luggage you have?" Drew stared at her large denim shoulder bag and single small suitcase. She glanced down at her baggage.

"All expenses paid right?"

"Yeah, I just thought you being a woman..."

Beth gave him a glaring stare when he said this.

"Oh, never mind," Drew said, in an attempt to not put his foot any further into his mouth.

From the apartment they took a taxi to the airport and got onto a plane. Beth held onto Drew as the plane left the ground.

"Are you all right?" He asked her as she squeezed his arm.

"I've never flown before." She replied with a frightened tone in her voice.

"You should have told me," he said with a slight chuckle. He then took her other hand and held it as the plane climbed high into the air.

Once the plane reached cruising altitude Beth calmed down. Jack ordered a drink and Rich followed Jack's lead, soon ordering a drink as well.

Drew hoped Cindy might begin to socialize with Beth on the plane but instead Cindy also soon had a drink in hand and paid no attention to Beth who sat across the aisle from her.

He did come to enjoy the take off and landings of the flights. He would hold Beth's hand and she held his arm tightly.

Since Cindy ignored Beth for the most part, Drew focused on keeping her company. When he wasn't talking to her she would pull her Candace Clarendon book out and read quietly.

After several flights the group found themselves walking down mobile stairs in order to depart their plane at the Fairbanks Alaska airport. The airport seemed a bit old-fashioned and out of date, but Jack, having indulged in a number of drinks; on as well as off the planes, reveled in the atmosphere.

"Now we're in the wild," he exclaimed loudly as he walked down the stairs, holding his arms up and presenting the small airport and the obvious wilderness in the background to his fellow companions.

Drew thought he'd packed modestly but as he examined Beth's small amount of baggage he felt a bit embarrassed that his luggage required two hands to carry rather than one arm.

Once inside the airport, Jack made a call from a pay phone and directly a small van taxi picked them up and off they went.

The hotel they arrived at certainly wouldn't be considered five star accommodations, but Drew realized in the wilderness setting of Fairbanks it would be sufficient. Also, this must be the best available since Jack had paid.

The following day Jack moved from room to room getting everyone up and around. He seemed to thrive on being a boss. Drew actually thought of him as being bossy on these trips rather than being much of an actual leader. Jack just told everyone what to do without much thought or more often than not with an alcohol induced thought behind it. As the benefactor for these trips however, Jack assumed total control and this fact often concerned Drew.

Putting his glasses on, Drew stepped into the hall followed by Rich. Soon Beth stepped out of her room. He admired Beth in her shorts and tiny tee shirt. Strange, he thought, even this early in the morning she almost glowed. Maybe he was falling in love; he turned away before she noticed him watching her.

The warm feeling Drew had about Beth concerned him some. As he got ready, he thought about it. He'd never been in love before. Even in high school he was the guy who simply fell flat on his face when dealing with girls. His failed attempts to flirt with the young women he'd liked in high school echoed in his mind like sad songs, long overplayed.

Now the feeling he had for Beth was like a warm fire inside his heart. He wouldn't let anything harm this wonderful relationship developing between them. This was something special and he would treat it as a delicate flower that he must tend to gently and patiently.

After a quick breakfast the group moved outside and found a large van waiting. Three brand new, bright red, double seated kayaks sat on a trailer connected to the van. After some admiring and touching of the new kayaks, the group began loading their bags in the vehicle. Jack spoke with the driver and loaded his bag last. After a short drive they arrived at an outfitting store.

"All right gang," Jack instantly took the lead role, "here is a list of stuff we must have and if you think of anything else, go ahead and get it. However, keep in mind there's not much room in a kayak."

Inside the store everyone rounded up sleeping bags, tents , etc. One of the items on the list Drew and Beth received was 'one hundred feet of nylon rope.'

Drew moved over to Beth as she admired a light blue coat.

"You may need that." He said.

Beth smiled.

"I didn't bring much money, so I'll do without."

He took the jacket from her hand and examined the front, and back; then he held it up to Beth.

"Yes, I'm absolutely sure now," he said.

"Sure of what?"

"This coat, I noticed as I held it up to you, no one else would be as beautiful in it as you would." When he said this Beth laughed a little and this made Drew smile also.

"Well, I'm not going to ask Jack to spend anymore money on me. I don't want to take advantage of him."

Drew gave her a silly face. "No, no, I certainly don't want you to take advantage of Jack. In fact I'm going to buy some things for you just to make sure if anyone gets taken advantage of by you, it'll be me! Call me crazy Beth, but I kind of enjoy the thought of you taking advantage of me."

Beth gave him the sad smile he loved, then laughed as Drew laughed along with her.

"Hey, what's going on over there?" Rich shouted from several racks over.

"I'm working on a method for Beth to take advantage of me," Drew replied with some excitement.

"Oh, well never mind, forget I asked," Rich walked in the opposite direction and this caused Beth and Drew to laugh even more.

Drew found a coat his size; similar to the one she'd picked out and soon everyone gathered together outside, ready to go. The group loaded into the van and off they went again.

As they drove out of Fairbanks the wilderness closed in around them. Soon moose could be spotted from time to time grazing on the side of the road. Rich seemed to almost jump out of the window when he spotted a black bear with several young bears in tow.

After several hours of driving, the van pulled off the highway and up to several log buildings. Two older style gas pumps stood outside and a sign over the larger of the two buildings read "Eagle Ridge

Trading Post." About twenty yards behind the buildings a river could be seen. The group got out of the van; looked around and stretched.

In front of the trading post the parking area fairly well amounted to rock, gravel and some random mud holes. Trees and brush embraced the isolated speck of humanity. The driver of the van started backing the trailer down the brushy trail to the river once everyone had disembarked.

"Last stop before the river run," Jack said, seeming to be energized now that danger permeated the atmosphere. He continued, "If you want or need anything else, such as feminine unmentionables or such, this would be the place to take care of that."

"Let's go browse a bit shall we?" Drew said to Beth. She nodded. Together they walked up to the trading post. As they entered the door an old fashioned doorbell connected to the top rang out.

The aroma inside consisted of cut wood, a wood stove and a variety of foods, meats, leathers and several smells that Drew couldn't quite identify. He realized this must be an old establishment yet it was well built.

As the two progressed through the store they passed souvenir T-shirts, coats, hats and other Alaska items. On the opposite side of a checkout counter was an elderly lady, but she stood tall and seemed to be very fit despite her apparent age.

Behind the woman, on the wall, hung a number of antique items such as snowshoes, and a harpoon as well as some harpoon tips that appeared to be fashioned from bone. In between the large array of Alaskan artifacts stood a shelf and on this shelf rested many smaller assorted artifacts, all arranged neatly for display.

Beth gazed at the items with interest; her mouth slightly open as if the shiny trinkets held her spellbound. Drew glanced over at her and immediately thought of a child examining the flavor list on the side of an ice cream truck.

He then followed an invisible line from her eyes, to identify which item had captured so much attention from her. On a center shelf, in the middle of the various antiques, stood a small red bottle with what looked to be faded ivory decorations around the outside.

While this took place the elderly lady moved to the end of the counter to do what Drew would call busy work.

"You kids are going out on the river a little late in the year aren't you?" The woman seemed to be asking though she never looked up from her dusting and organizing.

"Yes, I suppose we are," Drew replied as he moved closer to Beth. Then a thought occurred to him while standing beside her.

"Excuse me, could we see the little red bottle on the middle shelf?" When Drew asked the lady this Beth seemed to awaken from her trance.

"What are you doing?" She spoke in a whisper and as if a bit embarrassed by his request. The woman came over to the counter and picked up the bottle, then handed it to Drew. He held the bottle in his hand for a few seconds and noticed Beth's eyes light up. She moved very close to him as he examined the delicate item.

"What a beautiful little bottle," was all she said.

The small glass container had a deep, almost glowing red color. What appeared to be faded ivory had been fashioned on the outside and the distinct outline of a tiger or large cat could be made out around it in a delicate fashion.

Drew thought the ivory must surely have been hand carved and the bottle itself certainly very old.

"That particular bottle is an antique Chinese snuff bottle, from what I've been told over the years. Supposedly it came from Whisper," the old woman said as she watched them admiring it.

"Whisper?" Beth turned to the old woman with an apparent lack of understanding.

"Yes, Whisper. It's something of an Atlantis in these parts. Some people think the place really exists and others say the story is another Alaskan tall tale from the gold rush days.

"That little bottle I received as a gift from my uncle around, oh, maybe twenty years ago. He worked for the forestry service and according to him a hiker stumbled out of the woods almost half dead. He gave it to my uncle after telling him the bottle had come from Whisper."

"So, is Whisper a town or...?" Drew asked, becoming very interested by this time.

"I suppose we would call it a town, but then we call a congregation of ten people and five dogs a town around here," the woman said smiling.

"The story, from what I've heard goes this way. Back during the gold rush days two brothers by the name of Janik and Felix Varga came to Alaska searching for gold. No one really noticed when they arrived as they came along with hundreds of others. How long the two struggled in the Alaskan wild is also unknown.

"They turned up one day in Fairbanks, straight from the wilderness, carrying with them almost pure gold nuggets, some of which they promptly sold for tickets back to the States. This is, of course when they became noticed.

"Most of the people that did take notice however had forgotten about the brothers or moved on by the following spring when the two returned to Fairbanks. But, a few remembered the gold nuggets they possessed the previous year and decided to follow them to locate the rich find.

"The brothers must have been aware of this possibility and put a plan together. They rented an old store building on the edge of town.

Over the next several weeks their family and close associates arrived in Fairbanks five and ten at a time.

"The activity around the old store building picked up as the people connected to the Varga group arrived. It wasn't long before a small group of swindlers desiring to find the brothers gold began to keep an eye on the group.

"First they tried to get information from people in the group. None of the party said anything however, and for the most part they would aggressively brush off the 'would be' claim jumpers.

"Some of the spies tried to follow the brothers in an effort to locate the mysterious location. The Varga brothers must have also foreseen this though as they would separate and move about at all hours of the day and night. They slyly evaded their pursuers again and again. During this time people began to speculate, and as the Varga group grew larger and became more elusive in their affairs, a kind of pre-legend began to grow around them. I don't suspect anyone at that time foresaw what was about to happen.

"After weeks of continual activity around the old rented store building; someone noticed the Varga group had vanished. All the people desiring to horn in on the brothers gold were sorely disappointed when they arrived at the old store building to find the tents still up but not a soul to be found.

"The consensus eventually came down to two theories concerning their disappearance. The first theory was that the group had a preset date to move. Then, possibly during a brief night, they all moved quickly from Fairbanks and no one noticed.

"The second theory and the one that seems most likely, is that small groups left until only a few were around. These few went about tending numerous campfires and creating the impression of there still being a large group at the store building. Then this small group slipped away at a convenient moment."

At this point the woman had to stop and tend a customer. After a moment she returned. Drew and Beth stared at her intently. She appeared to be having trouble recalling her thoughts. Then she asked.

"So where was I?"

Beth replied quickly.

"The Varga group vanished from Fairbanks."

"Oh yeah, that is correct." The woman said, as she re-established her train of thought.

"So anyway, the entire Varga operation looked to be a complete success at first. Everyone seemed to have been totally surprised by the Varga's ability to keep complete secrecy.

"Then, finally, after a week or so of absolute darkness on the matter, a young boy surfaced to shed a little bit of light on the group's disappearance.

"This young boy as it turns out, had been playing with one of the Varga brother's nieces. She made him promise not to tell anyone before she would reveal anything to him. And it was with some reluctance that the young lad gave any information.

"When he did finally speak on the matter, he said the young girl told him she and the others were moving to a secret location her uncles had found for them. Once there, they would build a town. Her uncles had already named the town Whisper. She also informed the boy that everyone in the town would become rich."

At this point the woman stopped. Drew and Beth both stared at her in anticipation.

"So what happened?" Drew finally asked.

"No one knows," she said as if she had been looking for another starting point. "The Varga group disappeared into the wilderness of Alaska and no one knows what happened to them."

"Didn't anyone look for them?" Beth asked.

"Sure they did, in fact a few years later some relatives of the people who left with the brothers sent detectives and scouts to search for their loved ones.

"As a result of these inquiries and an investigation by local authorities, a gold stake claim surfaced which the Varga brothers filed before leaving. But when the area of this claim was searched, the result came to nothing but open wilderness. A theory came to be that either the brothers simply filed a worthless claim to throw off any pursuers or they were confused themselves as to the exact location according to a map."

"So, everyone just gave up looking for them?" Drew asked with a bit of disbelief.

The woman took a slow deep breath before continuing. "No not really; actually there's been people looking for Whisper ever since the Varga group showed up with the gold nuggets. And many of them have just disappeared as well. No one knows how many explorers and gold hunters have vanished in the Alaskan wilderness while searching for Whisper.

"You should also keep in mind the time frame we're talking about. When the Varga group disappeared, Alaska could only be searched by ground and maybe to some extent by river. With the sheer size involved, any search would be difficult as well as possibly deadly for searchers.

"This isn't your average wilderness and you kids should get your little canoe trip wrapped up before the snow starts. I strongly suggest you get back into civilization within a couple of weeks. If the snow comes early you could get into real trouble."

"Yes, we plan on being out a few weeks and no more," Drew said, and then after a slight pause continued.

"I wonder if you would be interested in selling this bottle."

The old woman looked at Drew a little strangely.

"Well, young man, everything in this building is for sale, but you should know, I'm quite fond of that little bottle."

"That is fair warning. Let's talk about price."

Drew and the woman negotiated for a while, but eventually he got the bottle.

"I can't believe what you paid for that bottle," Beth exclaimed as they walked out the door. "You must have really wanted it."

"As a matter of fact I did," Drew said with a sly tone. He stopped and Beth stopped. "I wanted to get you something very special Beth and that jacket is not nearly special enough. I bought the bottle for you."

Drew handed the small sack with the bottle to Beth. She took the small package and clasped it in her hands as if it were a kitten or small treasure. Several tears immediately began welling up in her eyes and she turned her head down to avoid Drew seeing her cry.

"No one has ever done anything like this for me." She said, trying to speak through the tears.

Drew gently lifted her head with his hand under her chin. He gazed into her eyes and then wiped a tear from her cheek. She smiled and then laughed and almost cried at the same time.

"Come on now, a beautiful girl like you, I find that a little hard to believe. But at least I know now this is the special something I've been looking for, and that's a good thing." He said softly as she hugged the small sack.

"Beth, I want to do more than just buy you a present." As Drew said this Beth became serious and gazed into his eyes. Realizing he wanted to tell her something special she listened closely.

"I want to be the man that changes everything for you. I want to be the man you can count on; the one that will be there when you need me to be there. Beth, I promise you here and now that I'll be there for you when you need me. I won't ever let you down."

He paused for a few seconds and Beth wrapped her arms around him in an embrace. Drew ran his hand over her brown hair and continued.

"In fact, when we get back I would like for you to get an apartment closer to me. In the same complex if possible; I'd feel better. I'll help you with the finances. I really want you to be closer and, well, I would just feel better."

Beth looked up at him. She studied his face for a few seconds and put her head back on his chest.

"I just don't know if I'm ready for that Drew. I know you're concerned. I'll think about it, all right?" She again looked up to him. Drew nodded to her.

She then gave Drew a quick kiss on the lips. She pulled the bottle from the sack and admired it briefly. Drew smiled as she appeared happy. She then put the small bottle into a pocket of the jacket he'd bought for her earlier.

Drew felt a flash of excitement run through his body from head to toe. He was now glad they came on the trip.

As the two walked arm in arm to the river they could see Jack and Cindy standing beside the van talking. Rich busily packed the front of his two man kayak with supplies.

"Come on you two love birds, we need to get on the water," Jack yelled out as he pulled a map from his pocket.

Drew felt flush with confidence after his success with Beth.

As they came closer Drew said. "Before we get on the water, could you please tell us the plan?"

Jack turned to him, expressing some surprise at this type of remark coming from Drew.

"Well, my good man, and fair lady, the plan is quite simple." Jack unfolded the map across the hood and windshield of the van. "We simply get on the river right here, and travel straight down to Jackson Point right there."

After Jack said this, Cindy, rather snidely, commented. "There's nothing simpler than that." She then strolled off towards the kayaks with a few small items in her hands.

Drew, not quite as impressed as Cindy, took a closer look at the map.

"Yeah, I see the river runs down to Jackson Point, but what about all of these branches in the river, if we get on one of those we'll end up out in the middle of the Alaskan wilderness."

Jack smiled at Drew, as if he had just called him on a poker hand.

"That's a sharp observation Drew, but if you'll notice, as long as we stay alert and always stay to the right and not venture off on any of the left forks, we'll remain on the major river run."

Drew and Beth studied the map a few seconds.

"Okay," Drew replied, "I see you've got a thought out plan, that's all I needed to know."

Jack flashed an arrogant smile, folded up the map and then walked up to the trading post as Drew and Beth packed gear into their kayak.

The driver moved the van away from the river and the group waited for Jack.

Soon he could be seen heading back towards the river, stumbling a bit as if he'd been drinking a bit too much already. He had a bag cradled in his left arm.

He stopped and talked with the driver of the van for a few moments. Then came on down to the river as the van pulled away.

Everyone watched Jack as he tried to put the bag into him and Cindy's kayak. There wasn't enough room. He came over to Drew and Beth.

"Put this in your kayak would you?"

Drew could hear the glass bottles inside the bag and knew the contents must be some type of booze.

"We don't have room Jack." Though Drew didn't want to take the booze at all, he did speak the truth about not having room.

"Nonsense," Jack dug around in the kayak and pulled out a bag. "What's this?"

Drew looked at the bag. "That's a hundred feet of nylon rope."

Jack threw the bag up on the river bank.

"After some thought, I've realized this rope won't be required after all." He then put the bag in the spot where the rope had been. "All right, let's move out," he said and moved over to his kayak.

CHAPTER THREE: INTO THE WILD

Beth had no experience in a kayak, but Drew had sufficient kayaking skills for both of them.

He'd always seemed to be the least capable of the group before this trip, as Jack, Cindy and Rich were all natural outdoors people. Yet he now felt a renewed confidence around Beth.

Even though she'd never been in a kayak, she listened to Drew and soon became fairly capable on the water. Drew sat behind her and admired her beautiful brown hair as much as he did the scenery.

She reacted as a child visiting the zoo for the first time. Beth examined the trees and wildlife with an excited enthusiasm that prompted Drew to enjoy it all even more as well. When a moose or bear appeared on the river bank she would turn back to him with a smile that warmed his heart and caused him to react with a smile in return.

After several days on the river Beth almost seemed to be at a loss for words as the pristine scenes floated by. A bald eagle swooped from the sky in an attempt to catch a fish. Beth followed the great bird as it descended majestically. Then as the eagle flew back into the sky above them she simply said: "It's so beautiful isn't it?"

Drew smiled and replied. "Yes, you are."

She turned quickly and gave him a coy look. "Hey, what are you watching anyway?"

They both smiled and laughed a little. Drew felt at this moment he must be falling in love with Beth.

The sheer magnitude of Alaska managed to capture everyone's attention. The vast forest and unbridled river immediately put the group into the surreal sensation of being in another world, or at least in a place no one had ever seen before. No trace of people could be seen anywhere. To Beth, who hadn't spent much time in the outdoors and certainly nothing such as this, Alaska prompted a love for nature she never realized could be stirred in her.

The others in the group took on a rugged outdoor persona as the wilderness enveloped them. Drew however didn't seem to react in an artificial manner.

Beth attempted to think of herself as an outdoor person. She didn't feel right though knowing she had much to learn and quickly stopped thinking such a thing.

She increasingly found solace in Drew as he simply enjoyed being in the pristine wilderness with someone he cared for.

They often stopped to camp on small river islands. Jack determined these types of islands, when available, would be a little safer from bears and such. As the trip progressed, Beth also noticed that it didn't really get dark at night but rather the light simply grew faint.

Over the days the weather slowly became more overcast with clouds. This prompted Beth and Drew to wear their new jackets more often as the temperature also turned more cold, especially in the evening.

Drew and her began to cuddle up more. She would sit closer to him by the campfires. He began to put his arm around her during these occasions and she didn't seem to mind.

Drew found himself daydreaming more often. With Beth sitting close to him he could imagine them having a small house. They would watch TV in the afternoon and she would cuddle with him on the couch. It became a little difficult at times for him to leave this hopeful future of Beth and him together.

His words concerning Cindy turned out to be quite accurate. Cindy showed little interest in getting to know Beth or even associating with her for that matter.

Beth initially admired Cindy as being pretty. She thought Cindy's light brown, almost blonde hair to be fantastic and liked the way she kept it tied back in fashionable styles.

Cindy's athletic nature would have also impressed Beth more if not for the fact she wielded it arrogantly. Rather than assisting her, she would chuckle when Beth did something wrong and react as if she were a child.

Eventually Beth simply stayed close to Drew and gave Cindy little of her attention. Under these circumstances she became a bit surprised when Cindy asked her a question after setting up camp on one of the river islands.

"So Beth, we heard you and Drew met in the college library. What's your major?"

She gazed across the campfire at Cindy and then turned to Drew as if he might provide her with an appropriate response.

"Well, I uh...," she appeared to be stuck.

"Do we have to talk about school while we're on vacation?" Drew said and then turned and smiled slightly at Beth, who smiled back; seeming glad he intervened.

"Oh boy Drew, you're in trouble." Jack quickly responded after taking a drink from his small bottle.

"What do you mean?"

"Well, you're not fooling me. I know why you two don't want to talk about school." Jack paused and Beth again turned to Drew with a concerned gaze.

"She's an Art Major of course. Only an Art Major wouldn't want to talk about school."

Drew chuckled a little when Jack said this and Beth smiled slightly.

Jack continued.

"Like I said Drew, you're in trouble. You'll be paying rent on some art shop that never makes any money and probably be supporting some poor unemployed art students who think their lousy paintings should be worth a million dollars."

Jack, Cindy and Rich laughed and Drew and Beth laughed a little as well.

"You've really got the 'Art Major' stuff figured out don't you Jack?"

Jack peered across the campfire at Drew. With slightly slurred speech he replied, "You bet I do."

The five explorers continued on, making their way down the river and camping when a secure spot could be found. Jack as usual stayed on the bottle most of the time. When they would locate a camping spot Jack would generally be inebriated or on the verge. Cindy would reluctantly put the tent up and occasionally help gather some wood to get the fire going.

Drew and Beth had separate single tents but would put them close together. Rich generally slept on the ground in his sleeping bag and seldom bothered to put his tent up.

Their food supply came in individual packages. This happened to be one of the things Jack did do well in the preparation department. As things turned out, even with the individual packages the group received a bear visitor on one occasion, searching for food. Jack Pulled out a horn attached to an air canister and the loud blast ran the bear off. After the initial fright wore off the group had a good laugh.

"What would you guys do without me?" Jack said and now began to strut around even more than before.

"I see what you mean about Jack being overconfident." Beth said under her breath, and then moved a little closer to Drew as if avoiding Jack's arrogance.

A week into the trip the group considered themselves to be old hands at setting up camp. Beth and Drew also felt confident in their abilities to see the trip through. With a lack of sunshine the cold from the water and the ground became more intense. A hazy mist began to develop over the river. This mist settled and everything had dampness from what felt to be more than a fog but less than what might be called drizzle.

Their travel down the water moved along unimpeded and for the most part on the schedule Jack had set for them.

Then, ten days out from the Eagle Ridge trading post Beth spotted something that would change everything.

"What's that over there?" She pointed to the bank as the kayaks slid effortlessly down the river. Drew turned to the area where Beth pointed and could see what appeared to be a small stone pyramid a few yards up on the bank of the river.

"Hey, you guys see that. What is it?" He pointed as well, and then steered their kayak towards the object of interest.

As the others noticed the strange mound they also moved towards the river bank. After reaching land they tied their kayaks up and walked to the strange mound of rocks.

"This has to be man made, there's no doubt about that." Drew didn't claim to be an archeologist, but he felt certain to be the most knowledgeable of the bunch. The mound of rocks stood around four feet high and had a base of about four to five feet.

"I wonder who put this here and how long ago." Cindy said as she studied the odd discovery.

The strange assemblage of rocks presented something completely out of place after ten days of nothing but virgin wilderness. Then, when everyone had become quiet Beth noticed something else.

"Do you hear that?" She held up her hand to silence any possible comments. She peered into space as if trying to pull the sound from the air. Everyone listened intently for what she spoke of.

For several moments the five stood motionless trying to detect what Beth indicated she heard. Then Jack broke the silence.

"Just what are we listening for?"

"I can hear something from that direction; like people talking." Beth pointed to the right of the direction they had been traveling and across to the woods.

"I don't hear anything," Cindy said rather gruffly.

"I don't either," Jack said. "What about you guys?" Jack looked at Drew and Rich. Rich shook his head no. Drew, not wanting to leave Beth by herself said he heard something though he couldn't make out what.

"Maybe we're close to a village," Drew added, hoping something would transpire rather than Beth becoming embarrassed.

"We're still days away from any civilization," Jack replied without hesitation.

"So, what exactly do you hear?" Cindy asked.

"I can hear what sounds like people talking, or maybe whispering, but it's very faint and seems to be a long ways away."

"Should we go check it out," asked Rich.

Jack turned towards the woods and in the direction Beth had pointed.

"No," he said, "I don't think we should get away from the river. If we head off into the woods we could get lost."

"Maybe you're hearing an animal or the wind making the sound similar to a person's voice." Drew said.

Beth thought for a few seconds and replied. "Yeah, maybe that's what it is."

"All right then," Rich perked up and sounded happy that a resolution had been made. "Let's go, if everyone's ready."

The five made their way back to the kayaks. Once they started moving farther down the river, the sounds became clearer to Beth. Then as they came upon a small branch on the same side as the mound of rocks, Drew heard the sounds Beth spoke of.

"I hear it now," he yelled out. "Listen, it's coming from that direction." Drew pointed off to the right, and up the small river branch.

"I hear it too," Rich said and he steered off into the branch.

Since Rich happen to be in front, the other two kayaks fell in behind him. The woods and tall hills closed in on the sides of the group as the branch appeared similar to a large creek in comparison to the expansive river. Though narrow it remained deep, and as the group moved along the side of a large hill and around several bends the sounds became more audible.

After paddling up the branch, a while they rounded another small bend and Beth yelled out, "The sound is coming from over there" and pointed up to a hill. The three kayaks slowed to a crawl as they slowly paddled to keep from being moved back towards the river. Drew agreed with Beth that he could hear the sounds coming from somewhere along the hill to their left.

Cindy also said she could hear the sounds and Jack finally heard the strange sounds after listening intently for a few seconds.

At first, nothing seemed odd about the hill that the sounds came from. The group came to the edge of the water and held onto limbs and roots as Drew examined the hill. As he moved up to the edge of the water he noticed something out of the ordinary.

"Look at where the tops of those trees are and then look up the hill from those," he pointed about mid-way up the hill and about a quarter mile distance. Strangely, the hill didn't appear to be complete from what they could see.

Examining the hill closer they realized some type of ravine must cut into the hill, which from the river branch, was very difficult to distinguish. As they followed the tree lines down and moved along side of the hill, the group came to a point where two trees lay across each other. This initially appeared to be solid ground due to vegetation, moss, and roots growing thick on the long dead trunks.

Drew investigated the downed trees closer. He noticed they'd obviously laid in this position for a long time due to an abundance of plants having taken up residence all over the two massive hulks.

"What's this," he said pointing to the bottom of the two huge trunks. As the group peered through the vegetation hanging on and around the fallen giants, water could be seen streaming from underneath them. Moving closer they noticed a rather large gap present from behind the trees along the bank and where other tree tops could be seen on the other side of the downed trees and vegetation.

Drew continued moving closer into the thick vegetation when he suddenly shouted. "Hey, you have to see this!"

He realized that once through the initial vegetation there was a gap between the water and the tree trunks. Beth lowered her head as Drew maneuvered their kayak underneath the large trees and they disappeared behind them.

"Hold on there little Buckaroo," Rich yelled as they moved through the vegetation. He then immediately paddled quickly along the path Drew and Beth went and soon he'd disappeared behind the vegetation also. Jack and Cindy then maneuvered their kayak underneath the large tree trunks and hanging vegetation.

As they moved from underneath the fallen trees, plants and roots, the three kayaks slipped into a narrow but fairly deep stream that ran along the side of the hill. On their right, a steady increase in land; the ravine ran along the river on the other side. This could cause the ravine to be almost undetectable from this branch of the river.

The trees growing on the right side continued to get thicker as the group moved along the stream and the land separating the stream from the river branch continued to increase. Soon they had moved far enough along that they could no longer identify how far away from the river branch they were. Then a sharp bend in the stream moved them into an open area that cut into the hill.

At this moment the sun almost broke through the clouds. This caused the ravine to brighten a bit as the explorers entered. They gazed along the line of a woodland canyon in the hillside, which moved upwards in something of a step fashion. A number of old log cabins could be seen nestled along both sides. And at the bottom could be seen the remains of a once very active stream. The water became more shallow as the party moved into a small lagoon area.

Drew could visualize the natural causes of this hidden area in the forest. At the upper part of the ravine a fast flowing stream, possibly even a small river branch at one time. The water flow would have cut out the large area from the hillside as it made its way along the hill until merging with the larger river branch. As the stream became weak over time, it left a large hidden space unseen from the river branch.

As the three kayaks floated slowly into the small lagoon no one spoke except Rich who simply said. "Wow."

Pulling up to the shallow end, they got out of the kayaks and began looking around for a place to tie them. Eventually they decided to run the lines of two of them through the line of one and daisy chain them together. This solution meant only the one kayak had to be tied to the tree stump on the bank. Then the group began exploring. Immediately Rich located something of interest.

"Look at this guys, oh and gals." In the brush along the edge of the lagoon bank laid two long boats turned upside down. Holes gaped in the bottoms; they had long since deteriorated beyond being water worthy. The boats heralded from a time the group had only seen in black and white photos.

"How old do you suppose these are?" Rich asked.

Drew examined the boats. "From what I can tell they're probably from around the turn of the century, maybe a hundred years old, what's left of them."

The five moved on towards the next elevation of the ravine. To get there they found remnants of an old trail. As the group reached this second level, a somewhat open area about the size of a small baseball field came into view.

Drew pointed out the trace of where the stream had flowed and caused a natural pool, then receded leaving a relatively flat open area. A few small trees grew in this area but a short bushy grass seemed more prevalent.

They decided to make camp here and soon had the tents pitched.

CHAPTER FOUR: PATHS OF THE FORGOTTEN

B eth stood viewing the cabins farther up into the ravine. Having finished putting their tents up Drew eagerly came to her side.

"You think anyone still lives in those cabins?" she asked.

He turned to the structures in the distance. "No, I don't think anyone has lived around here for a long time. From what I can see the cabins have been built with logs from cedar trees, or spruce maybe, but defiantly coniferous evergreens; they're all over this area. Those trees naturally repel insects; other types of wood, insects would have increased rot and decay."

"You see the windows," Drew pointed at a cabin and a small window that faced them. "The windows are small and made from the same wood, not from glass. This enabled them to better keep out the extreme cold during the winter. I suspect by having wood rather than glass windows the cabins remained more closed up and potentially may have helped preserve them."

Beth slid her arm around his waist. This surprised him at first and he felt a little awkward but he then put his arm around her waist and they stood together enjoying the moment.

"I wonder if this is the place the lady at the trading post told us about."

Drew glanced down at Beth as he seemed to suddenly recall the elderly lady's tale.

"I suppose it could be. It would certainly explain the name of Whisper."

Rich seemingly came from nowhere. "Do you believe this? It's like, the lost world or something!" He obviously had few reservations about their find and appeared ready to conquer the mysterious surroundings with his usual gusto.

"I'm not so sure about a lost world," Beth replied. "I think it looks more like a ghost town. This place is spooky. Where is that sound coming from?" She seemed to almost shiver after saying this and pulled herself even closer to Drew.

"Yeah, it's a ghost town," Rich said, seeming quite excited by the new prospect. "That's what it is, a ghost town! Spooky! How cool is that, we found an old ghost town!" He then more or less bounced off to share his excitement with Jack and Cindy.

The air felt colder and heavy with moisture as they sat around the fire later. The gray of the evening and night seemed to get grayer. The strange sounds continued to call out. Though Rich and Jack talked and joked loudly without concern; Beth still didn't appreciate the eerie sounds.

She gazed up towards the cabins and saw movement around the doors. She tried to reassure herself that it must be her imagination, or maybe a squirrel or small animal crawling about the old structures. Several times she turned away to prevent the fear inside her from taking hold.

The group decided they needed to rest before they explored the cabins. Rich wanted to investigate them right away but they'd been on the river all day and everyone except Rich expressed exhaustion.

Beth attempted to sleep in her tent but the mysterious sounds would come and go. Just as she would almost fall asleep the whispering would creep into her tent. A restless effort to rest persisted until she finally heard others moving around outside. She crawled out of her tent and saw everyone around the fire eating and talking.

"Well, good morning sunshine," Cindy said sarcastically.

Beth didn't bother to respond but instead went to the fire and held her hands close to warm them.

Jack already had a small bottle of something in his hand, taking drinks occasionally. Rich had what appeared to be only a few bites left of some type of food in a plate like dish. Drew came over by Beth and sat down on the ground beside her.

"So Beth, where did you say you were from originally?" Cindy gazed across the small fire with an arrogant expression.

"Tennessee," Beth replied, a little sleepily.

"Does everyone in Tennessee sleep this late?" Cindy said using a playful tone.

Jack smiled as he obviously thought Cindy's remark to be entertaining. Drew moved a little closer to Beth in an effort to express support.

"I really don't know Cindy. I haven't lived there for a long time."

This didn't seem to settle the matter for Cindy.

"Tennessee. Hmm. Isn't that where all the hillbillies come from?"

When Cindy said this Jack erupted in laughter and spewed his drink into the fire, causing a mini explosion. This in turn caused Rich to jump backwards, holding his plate up in an effort to not spill the remaining contents. Everyone except Drew and Beth burst into laughter.

Drew put his arm around Beth's waist and they watched the others until the situation settled back down.

"All right let's go," Rich said as he sat his empty dish down and then jumped up.

Beth pulled a granola bar from her jacket and opened it.

Rich had already started towards the next elevated area by the time the others began to follow. He moved to the side of the shallow stream as this appeared to be the easiest route. Before he ever attempted to move up towards the cabins however, he yelled loudly and bent down to the stream.

"What in the world?" Drew became startled by the yell and reacted as if his friend may be injured. The pace of the four quickened to catch up to Rich, who now labored beside the water.

As they approached Rich, he held something up in his hand. "Is this what I think it is? Look at this; it's all over the place, look in the water and along the sides of the stream."

Drew expressed some aggravation that he had hurried for no real emergency. But he pulled the item from Rich's hand and examined it closely.

"Well," Rich stared at Drew with a big smile, "is that what I think it is?"

Beth attempted to get a glimpse of what Drew now studied.

"It's a gold nugget," Drew finally said as he moved his hand up and down slightly in an effort to guess a weight. "Feels like a once or maybe even two," he added after a few seconds.

"Whoopee!" Rich yelled at the top of his lungs and caused Beth to jump as she still had her attention on the nugget in Drew's hand.

"We're going to be rich, rich, rich! Or my name isn't Rich...... and it is."

The others now began to examine the water. Without much searching they could see shining gold nuggets with interwoven quartz; most of them were the size of pecans and a few were the size of walnuts.

Drew began picking them up and putting some in his pockets. Beth followed Drew's lead and also began to pick the nuggets up and put them in her pockets. Rich worked feverishly and after his pockets became filled he began looking around for something to put more in.

"Does anyone have a bag we can use?"

No one said anything; instead they all continued to pick up the gold.

"Hey!" Rich yelled even louder trying to getting his friends attention. "Does anyone have a bag we can put this in?" Rich became frustrated standing with his hands full and no place to put the extra gold. Beth thought of the denim bag in her tent.

"Yes, I have a bag in my tent," she said barely looking up, "it's a heavy denim bag; it will be great for this, just pour the stuff inside it onto my sleeping bag."

Rich ran off towards the camp with his fists full of gold.

Beth searched for the nuggets along the banks of the stream as the water was extremely cold.

Rich came back with her bag and immediately went back to work filling it.

After around fifteen minutes, Jack and Cindy began to lose interest in digging around in the stream. Jack decided to walk back up to the cabins; Cindy followed behind him.

Beth could feel the weight in her pockets. She could carry the gold she now had without much difficulty but decided to stop before the weight became too cumbersome.

Drew also had his pockets as full as he wished to have them and began to move in the same direction as Jack and Cindy.

He glanced back at Rich. "Come on Rich, the gold isn't going anywhere. We'll get some more before we leave."

Rich seemed to pay little attention to what Drew said, but as he noticed the others moving towards the cabins he yelled out, "Hey! Guys wait for me. I want to put this gold up." He then trotted back towards the camp carrying the heavy bag thinking of how much more was still to be gotten.

Scanning over what must have been the community area, Drew counted seven buildings of various sizes, all made with large logs and log roofs that had moss and other light vegetation growing on them.

On a small level area and sitting in the brush, Drew could see remnants of what appeared to be an area used for wood cutting. A pile of old and weathered logs, to be used for building and the rusted end of a two man saw was spotted. Other assorted metal items, which he couldn't identify, lay interspersed, broken down and rusting away in the brush and trees.

One large building sat in what was the most level area. He thought the trees must have been cleared to build the cabins but over the years new ones grew and replaced them. The trees around the cabins appeared a little smaller than others in the area. Nevertheless, the woods surrounded everything and Drew realized this place would likely be impossible to spot from a plane, due to the natural camouflage.

The first cabin they came to sat nestled into the side of the hill. The structure remained generally intact as all of the buildings appeared to be. The long years revealed their toll by the result of the cabins settling into odd and irregular forms. Drew said this must be due to the "permafrost" the cabins sat on.

"The way it causes the cabins to set crooked really makes the place eerie," Beth noted as she examined the area. The small cabin they approached couldn't have housed many people, perhaps a small family. Jack pushed on the door and with reluctance and much scrapping on the floor the door moved open enough for a person to squeeze through. He peered into the old cabin and slid sideways into the ancient entry way.

The darkness only gave way to a dim light from the opening. Jack moved aside for Cindy to get through the door. Drew peeked in but didn't see much.

Inside, the cabin felt cramped to Jack and the odor of mold and earth permeated the air. A rough makeshift table sat in the middle of the room. To the side a bed or what remained of a bed resided against the wall. A fireplace presented itself from the side that adjoined to the hill, still holding remnants of a fire that died out long before any of the visitors had been born.

Propped up beside the fireplace the remains of snow shoes stood, as if waiting for the owner to return and tie them on. A rusted rifle perched above the fireplace, still awaiting the next hunt.

"Not much to see here," Jack said.

Cindy backed out and Jack came out behind her turning to walk towards the next building.

"Would you like to look inside?" Drew asked Beth.

She stepped in the doorway enough to get a look and then backed out. "It smells old," she noted and laughed a little. The two followed behind Jack and Cindy. Rich still far behind, climbing towards them.

The second cabin stood larger than the tiny one they first investigated. This cabin, though still small in comparison to a modern house, could possibly hold a family of four or five.

Trees had grown up right in front of this structure and in a strange gesture of nature reclaiming manmade objects; a single tree grew almost directly in front of the door.

Jack checked the windows and found them to be shut tight. Drew and Beth strolled around the outside, noting an area used for cutting wood and chuckling a bit when they rounded a corner to find a pile of vegetation that resembled the remnants of a wood pile prepared for the fireplace.

Finding little interest in this smaller cabin, they moved towards the next much larger cabin; by this time, Rich had jogged up to the others, breathing heavy from his efforts to catch up.

"Thanks for waiting for me guys," he said between breaths.

As the five came closer to the larger building the group slowly moved closer and once they'd climbed to the level area that the building sat upon, it became obvious this was indeed something other than a house-a lodge of sorts.

Though the trees had grown up around the building, the more central location and size indicated this to be an important structure for the community.

"Man, this is really wild," Rich said as they began to walk around it. The building seemed to be intact and in fairly good shape considering the years of endurance under the Alaskan sky.

In accordance with his nature, Jack went straight to the front door. He took hold of the crude handle and applied pressure from his entire body in anticipation of the door being difficult to open. To his and the others surprise the door opened easily and this almost caused Jack to fall inside the building.

As everyone stood outside observing Jack, the whispering sounds began again and could be heard clearly; much closer. Beth glanced up towards the sounds.

"That's where it's coming from," she said pointing to the top section of the long ravine.

From where they stood, a flat area with two poles was visible. In between the poles, what appeared to be a cave or entrance could be seen; a chill ran down Beth's spine as she gazed at the mysterious area.

"The sounds are like a bunch of voices all murmuring together," she said and pulled herself closer to Drew.

"Yeah," he replied looking in the direction of the sounds. "It's really weird isn't it? The only logical explanation is natural phenomenon. But when you listen closely it sounds like human voices."

When Drew said this, Beth examined his face closely as if to detect any fear. Drew appeared to have no doubt however that the sounds were from a natural source. She moved even closer to him and an involuntary shiver suddenly shook her.

After Jack moved into the log building, Cindy followed behind. Rich walked up to the door and peered in. Soon he stepped in and Drew and Beth followed closely, the last to enter into the building.

The dim light from outside barely lit the old structure. An open area with several rough tables and chairs sat immediately to the right as they walked in. The furniture seemed to be made from pieces of wood left over from the buildings. Though the tables and chairs were homemade and rough, they revealed themselves to still be in good condition as did the entire building.

"Hey, hey, what do we have here?" Jack said as he moved towards something of interest.

On the far side of the building a long counter resembling a tavern bar ran from the end to almost three quarters of the building. Behind the counter, on shelves, a multitude of very old supplies sat waiting to be purchased and used.

Behind the counter and towards the middle, a mirror hung on the wall. The mirror appeared rather small, though it may have just been small in comparison to the counter.

Jack examined the items behind the counter and found one area very interesting. As he sorted the items of interest, Drew moved inside and Beth came in behind him. Two small pot belly stoves sat about midway in each half of the building and the stove pipe ran up and then along the top of the building until it met the wall and went outside. On the wall at the end of the building a fireplace could be seen with wood stacked on each side, waiting in vain to release the stored energy still inside.

"There isn't as much of an old smell in this one," Beth noted and Drew nodded his head in agreement. Although the smell couldn't be described as fresh, it wasn't old and musky either. Beth wondered about this as she explored the interior.

"Well, now, I thought I might find something if I searched long enough," Jack now became excited as he shuffled bottles around behind the counter. Pulling a bottle from under the long table and then another he held them up in the dim light and peered into the caramel-colored liquid inside.

"Jackpot," he exclaimed loudly, "look here, this must be the good stuff."

Cindy strolled over and gazed into the bottles.

"Are you serious? Is that whiskey?"

"That is exactly what I believe is in these bottles my friends," Jack said with a large smile.

"That stuff must be a hundred years old," Cindy replied. "You can't actually drink that; can you?"

Jack came around the counter and sat the bottles down on one of the tables. He then sat down in one of the rough old chairs.

"Well, my dear, you are right about one thing, this stuff must be around a hundred years old," as he said this he seemed almost intoxicated by the mere vision.

Rich now sat down in one of the rough chairs beside Jack and also gazed into a bottle that sat close to him. "You're joking right; can this stuff still be good?"

Jack turned to him with a gleam in his eye. The others gathered around as Jack prepared himself to tell Rich something. He smiled and pointed at the top of the bottle.

"Still sealed," he said. "This is some fine aged liquor."

"Hey, why didn't the bottles freeze and break from the cold?" Rich asked suddenly.

Drew spoke up to answer Rich's question, "It's the alcohol content."

"Good answer!" Jack said. "Now who will take a drink with me?"

"Oh yeah," Rich replied with a smile as he handed Jack his multipurpose knife. "I will, but you have to go first Jack."

"Oh, you don't have to ask twice, my friend," Jack slapped Rich on the shoulder in a gesture of camaraderie.

Cindy went behind the counter and found some small shot glasses. She then went out to the stream and washed them while Jack opened one of the bottles. Drew and Beth sat down at a table next to the others.

"You two want in on this?" Jack still had a smile as he asked them.

"I don't drink," Beth said quickly.

"I'll pass as well," Drew added.

"All right, but you don't know what you're missing," Jack smelled the bottle cork as if it were a fine wine.

The dim light shining in through the open door presented a strange scene as Beth examined the interior. She felt as if a time warp had opened up and pulled her into it. Everything around her represented a century before hers and she became more apprehensive about this strange place they'd stumbled upon.

The whiskey must be of exceptional quality, Beth thought to herself, as the three drinking it became intimately involved in the two bottles after the first few drinks. The two who weren't drinking watched the drinkers for a few moments; then Drew and Beth got up and strolled around the building, amazed at the historic artifacts.

On the shelves behind the counter sat remnants of can goods, some had burst open from extreme cold and the contents long since dried up becoming nothing more than faint fragments of the original food inside.

Animal traps and ammunition aligned neatly along the shelves indicated this to be a town storeroom as well as the community tavern. They wandered around as they might in a museum, being careful to not damage anything and putting each item they choose to pick up back into its time weathered position on the shelf.

"I wonder what happened to the people," Beth said as they examined the items.

"That's a good question. It is possible..." Drew had to wait as the laughter of the three drinkers became loud for a few seconds. "It is possible," he said again, "an epidemic of some sort wiped the town out. That almost happened in Juno; I think it was Juno anyway, back in the nineteen twenties."

Beth considered this for a few seconds.

"But wouldn't there be skeletons," turning her head slightly at Drew while considering her question before adding, "the skeletons would still be here and the other cabins were empty as well."

"I suppose there should be," Drew said. "Maybe we've just not come across them yet. Or maybe most of the people were buried by the others until only a few were left and the remains of those are still in one of the cabins."

"I guess so," She replied, as her attention went back to the items on the shelf.

"Say, how about you and I go explore a bit more outside while those three drink themselves into a stupor."

She looked at Drew and smiled, "All right."

"You guys and gal have fun, we're going to go look around some more." Drew said as they walked past Jack, Cindy and Rich who were three sheets to the wind by now from the aged whiskey.

"Yes, you two do that," Jack said raising the almost empty bottle to the two, "and let us know if you find anything else exciting."

"Like more gold," Rich said rather loudly. "And don't be hogs if you do find more," he added.

Oliver Phipps

"I think there's enough around here for everyone," Drew replied as he ushered Beth through the door.

CHAPTER FIVE: SNARE, MY LOVE

Beth and Drew walked into the misty light and towards the shallow stream. In the water, a number of strategically located rocks created a crossing.

Gazing around, they could see another cabin on the other side of the stream and closest to the top of the ravine; had something unusual about it that immediately commanded their attention. Over the door, a very large set of moose or elk antlers hung majestically. This gave Drew the feeling this was a cabin of importance.

"Let's go check that one out."

"Okay," Beth replied.

They maneuvered over the stones to cross the waterway, and then began climbing towards the isolated cabin.

After a short climb, a level area occupied by a medium sized log cabin gave them a break. They looked the old structure over a bit but rather than trying to enter, they moved on towards the more interesting one further up the hill.

What appeared to be remnants of steps and a path cutting into the slope eased the remainder of their climb.

This cabin looked to be the best built of all the buildings. The roof of rough cut heavy logs had the usual moss and light vegetation growing on it as all the others had. The building also sat somewhat contorted due to settling over the years and this created the odd appearance of being built without using straight lines.

Looming above, the huge set of moose antlers rested over the door. The couple had seen moose as they traveled down the river, yet the size of the antlers had them guessing it must have been massive to carry such weight.

Drew lifted the latch on the door and pushed. Once again the two were surprised as this door opened without much effort. He peeked inside with caution, and then moved slowly in.

Beth stayed right behind him. Once the two stepped inside they strained to see by the dim light of the open doorway. After moving from the entrance, the light crept inside and presented an odd scene of animal antlers hanging on the walls and rough frontier style furniture. Walking around the picturesque cabin felt as if as they had invaded someone's home. Everything appeared to be waiting for the long lost owners return.

Beth giggled a little and pushed her hair from in front of her eyes as she examined crude dishes on a rough counter. She could barely imagine the time when anything other than modern plates and utensils were used.

As she moved down the counter an old camera came into view. Beside the old camera sat a metal box and on the wall above the counter a picture hung. Beth didn't touch the camera or box right away but instead examined the picture.

Dust and debris from years gone by covered the glass. She took the old picture down and gently wiped the glass off. Two men stood side by side in front of what looked to be a cave, one man had a beard and a dark colored shirt with suspenders, the other had a mustache with a light colored shirt and a black vest. She could see the men's similar features and close age they must be brothers.

The cave they stood in front of had roots streaming down from the trees above the mouth. On both sides of the men stood black totem poles about seven feet high with marking's around the mouths and eyes of the faces carved into the poles.

Drew meanwhile, slowly examined the single room of the old cabin with equal interest. One rough frontier style bed sat against the wall of one side of the room and on the far side another bed sat against the wall.

A canvas curtain, still hanging by threads, cordoned one of the corners. Peering into the small area Drew saw pans and bottles of chemicals and realized this had been used as a dark room to develop film.

As he continued to move around the room, getting closer to Beth, he noticed she held something in her hands and stared at it with great interest. He moved closer to her and as he came behind her she said, "I understand," as if talking to the picture. He looked over her shoulder and saw the picture of the two men.

"What do you understand?"

She looked back at Drew with a blank and almost emotionless face. Then she turned back to the picture.

"We should leave here Drew, we're not safe. I feel like," she paused as if to capture a feeling. "I feel like, we're being watched."

"Okay Sweetheart, we'll go back to the others."

"No, I mean this town, or village, whatever it is, the whole area; something's not right about this place. I think we should leave this area as soon as possible."

"Hey, I won't let anything happen to you." Drew put his arm around her. He thought she may have become spooked by the old picture, so he tried to present the artifacts in a more positive manner.

"One of the guys must have been a photographer." With some effort he picked up the very large antique camera, and then turned it slightly from side to side. He sat the camera back down and looked over the other items. "I suspect these are, or were, chemicals for developing film," he continued, pointing to several bottles against the wall behind the camera.

He then took hold of the metal box and gently opened it. Inside, a number of black and white pictures lay untouched for years. As the two pulled them out one by one from the box, each picture expressed a piece of an amazing story. There were people busily building a gold rush town and doing daily tasks. Pictures of snow covered trees and cabins, men and women working; large trees being cut down and children playing.

Drew stopped when he pulled up a picture similar to the one on the wall. Here the two men stood in front of the cave and one of them held a round item that resembled a large spider web. Yet this item appeared to be made by Native Alaskan people, from bones and other small items. Some of the bones were thin and spine like as if from a large fish or even a whale of some sort. Others resembled bones from creatures of the woods.

"That must be the cave the odd sounds are coming from," Drew said after examining the picture.

"What's that they're holding?" Beth asked.

"It looks like a native artifact. It resembles what's called 'dream catchers' back home. But that one is made from bones and animal skulls it seems. From what I know of these sorts of things, I would guess that's an item connected somehow to the cave behind them. Elaborately constructed pieces such as that would likely be used for ceremonial purposes."

Beth studied the photo as she might look at a crossword puzzle, her eyes lowered halfway and her lips closed together tightly as she seemed to absorb the scene.

"We should leave this place soon," she finally said under her breath.

The last of a handful of pictures in the box presented the two men sitting inside the large community building at the very same table Jack, Cindy and Rich sat at when Drew and Beth left them a few moments earlier.

A bottle and several glasses adorned the table in front of the two men. In the middle of the table however sat something that immediately caught Beth's eye. She quickly reached into the box and took hold of the picture. She then brought it close to her eyes.

"Look at that," she said pointing to a small bottle. Drew studied the picture and could plainly see the very same bottle they had purchased from the trading post a week and a half earlier.

"That's the antique snuff bottle I bought for you at the trading post." Drew exclaimed.

"It is," Beth said as she continued to stare at the picture, "which means, this must be Whisper."

"And those are the Varga brothers," Drew added.

"They've got to be." She patted her jacket in an effort to find the pocket holding the small bottle.

Just then Rich came stumbling into the open cabin door.

"Hey you two, come on, we're going to find out what's making that strange sound."

"You are drunk." Beth wasted no time identifying Rich's somewhat intoxicated state.

"I'm not drunk," stammered Rich. "Drew can you control your woman please?"

Drew made no reply but smiled at this statement; more because he liked Beth being called his woman than being amused at Rich's obvious state of intoxication.

"Come on you guys, Jack said I had to come up here to get you two."

Beth looked at Drew with concern.

"I don't really want to go Drew, I'm telling you there's something very wrong about this place, especially that cave or whatever it is up there."

"I understand, but if the other two are in the same state as Rich, we'd better go look after them. We'll let them take a quick look at the cave and then take them back to camp so they can sober up."

She said nothing, yet Drew knew from her expression she was reluctant to go, regardless of the reason.

Rich more or less bounced out the cabin door with Drew and Beth following behind. The three came up beside the stream where a path leading to the cave could be seen. Drew stopped and looked into the pool; and then he reached down into the water and pulled something out.

Beth walked up beside him and latching onto his arm, peeked at what he had pulled from the stream. Drew revealed a large gold nugget, interwoven with quartz... Rich now moved up beside Drew and noticed the nugget in his hand, which appeared to be about the size and shape of a large pecan.

"Man, we are going to be so stinking rich," he said gazing down at the nugget. Then he turned to the stream and began fishing around for another nugget of his own.

While the two examined the find, Jack called out from further up, around the area of the cave; gesturing with his arm for them to come up.

Drew handed the nugget to Beth and she put it in her pocket with the others. Then they climbed up the old pathway towards Jack and Cindy who were standing by the cave entrance.

As they came closer to the cave the whispering sounds became more pervasive. They reached the level area in front of the cave entrance where Jack stood with a bottle of whiskey in his hand.

Cindy meanwhile studied one of the totem poles at the front of the cave. The cavern appeared as it did in the photographs from the Varga brother's cabin, though the color of the totem poles had faded since the photos captured their likeness so many years earlier.

Roots draped the entrance, yet the definite mouth of a cave could be seen and they seemed to hang down like large strands of hair rather than completely obstructing the opening.

"What are these things?" Cindy asked in something of an intoxicated slur. Drew walked over to the totem pole she stood in front of.

"These are totem poles. The native people make these to indicate legends or stories, as well as metaphysical references; to mark what they consider spiritual or maybe sacred locations. Generally, tribes of the Pacific Northwest coastal areas produce totem poles. I would venture to say some of these people stumbled onto this location while hunting or exploring the rivers. Maybe the same way we did. However they found it though, it's obvious they decided to mark the location with these."

Drew moved closer to one of the totem poles and examined it from different angles.

"What seems strange to me though is that these are covered with tar or sap maybe."

"Why is that strange?" Beth asked.

"Well, I don't know a whole lot about totem poles, but I think when one is created it's sometimes painted in order to preserve it for a while, but not indefinitely. Whoever created these, must have intended for them to last a long time."

"If they felt like this was a dangerous place, maybe they put these here and wanted them to last as a warning?" She said.

"That's a possible reason I suppose," Drew replied, still eyeing the pole.

She stepped closer to Drew.

"Nothing about this place adds up. There's too many things wrong. I have a bad feeling about this place Drew."

He turned to her and could see the distress in her eyes. Turning back to the totem poles he examined them again; searching for something that might calm Beth's fears.

Jack turned up the bottle and a few bubbles gurgled up as he downed more of the vintage booze. Afterwards he wiped his mouth on his sleeve and almost shouted; "let's go see what all this mysterious noise is about." Then he walked straight into the cave pushing the roots aside as he went. Cindy turned and followed behind him without hesitation.

Beth took hold of Drew's arm.

"Don't go in Drew. I can feel it, we're being watched," she looked at him with eyes fixed in concern.

"I won't," he said, glancing around. Though he didn't see anyone watching them, he felt glad she was extremely concerned for his safety.

She let go of his arm after his reassurance and moved over to the other totem pole to examine it.

A few seconds after she let go of Drew's arm, Rich came up quickly from behind and grabbed him as a football player might. Then he shoved him into the cave opening yelling, "Come on you big puss, let's go see what's in this cave."

As Drew stumbled into the cave through the roots he looked back at Beth helplessly and raised his free arm as if to say, "What can I do?"

Beth took several steps towards the entrance raising an arm towards Drew in a vain effort to do something. Realizing she was about to pass through the totem poles she stopped instantly before stepping past the invisible boundary.

Once inside, but not far from the mouth of the cave, he and Rich met up with Jack and Cindy. Drew's eyes slowly adjusted to the dim light and he gazed around. He realized now that about four yards from the entrance a large room opened up.

The four moved cautiously towards the larger area. When they reached this open space Drew could see the top of the cave stood around eight feet high in a cathedral fashion, being rounded and peaked in the middle. The room itself was about twenty to twenty-five feet in diameter.

Along the sides, and attached to the wall were a number of the strange spider web looking artifacts. The craftsmanship of these native artifacts impressed Drew and he studied each one for a few seconds as they varied in shape, size, and style.

On the floor of the cave a number of the items lay in disarray and obviously worse condition than those on the wall; the apparent effects of being in the dirt for many years.

At the end of the enclosure and opposite the entrance, a rather large, oddly shaped hole was on the cave floor. From this hole came the mysterious sounds.

The whispering effect filled the cavern and flew about the four explorers like hummingbirds fluttering around their ears.

As Drew moved in different directions, he noticed the sounds would change in pitch and volume. He stood still and turned his head in an astonished manner at this discovery. Drew thought of how much the sound seemed human in characteristic.

Jack walked closer and examined the hole; squinting his eyes as if attempting to identify the source of the odd sounds. Cindy however carefully studied the odd artifacts on the wall.

After peering into the hole a few seconds and listening to the whispering sounds Drew moved over by Cindy in order to get another look at the artifacts on the wall.

Rich walked up beside Jack and motioned for the bottle in his hand. Seeming a little reluctant at first, Jack gave Rich the bottle and he quickly turned it up, taking a large drink.

"What are those Drew?" Jack asked, turning his attention to Drew and Cindy.

"My guess would be some form of talisman. These were possibly made by the local natives." Drew thought for a few seconds and continued. "From everything I've seen here I would theorize the natives of this area believed this to be a spiritual place or possibly that the phenomenon of the sounds from this cave were metaphysical in nature."

"You mean ghosts or demons; something along those lines?" Jack seemed more interested now but still managed to pull the bottle from Rich's hand after questioning Drew.

"Yeah maybe and these things would possibly be placed here to appease the spirits."

Jack took another drink and almost lost his balance in the process.

"You believe any of that stuff Drew?"

Jack put his free hand on Drew's shoulder as if he wanted a clear answer to his question.

Drew however suspected Jack of just needing something to hold onto so he wouldn't fall over. But, he played along and continued his analysis.

"I'm simply suggesting a theory based on the information available. There's obviously some reason for these items to have been placed here. But scientifically speaking, the hole and this cave must be the remnants of a small river from long ago.

"From a scientific perspective, this place has a reasonable explanation. The native Alaskans likely approached this place from a different frame of mind though. I'm simply suggesting that to be the reason these artifacts are here."

Drew pulled out from Jack's arm and went to the large hole.

"When I was a teenager, I thought I wanted to be a Geologist. I studied geology for several years and then got bored with it."

Drew gazed into the gaping hole a second.

"This is where a massive amount of water gushed out at one time, carving this cavern into the hill. Then the water moved out through the side of the hill here and a waterfall would have been out there." He motioned towards the mouth of the cave as he described the historic events.

"This area might be something similar to a huge geographical 'armpit.'" When Drew said this Rich laughed out loud and repeated the arm pit statement in a humorous voice.

"What do you mean by that?" Jack asked.

"Well, maybe that wasn't a great analogy, but the pressure from water, which somehow found its way out through this hill and then exited right at this point, is the same process that moved the gold from far underground to the surface and right out there into those pools."

Jack seemed to understand what Drew meant. He jumped into the conversation; trying to appear intelligent as well.

"So, way back, sometime long ago, where we're standing, a small river gushed up from that hole. And as the water moved out through that hole where the cave entrance is, it took the gold from underground along with it."

"That's correct," Drew replied and continued with his assessment.

"Then the water slowed down over time and eventually became a small stream leaving this hole and large amounts of gold out there in those pools of water," Drew moved his hand as if indicating the movement of the water and gold out the cave. Then he pointed back to the hole. "And this hole in the ground must have openings farther back into it somewhere, which with a little wind pushing through, causes the whispering sounds."

"So why did you call this place an armpit?" Rich asked.

"Well," Drew continued, "the strange configuration of this ravine along with the way the water cut into the hill caused this place to be very well hidden. The water cut out the ravine and created a pocket in the hill. But the water didn't cut through the hill and straight to the river. Instead, the water lost momentum at the bottom of the ravine then turned and moved along the side of the hill until merging with the river.

"Remember, when we came in, the stream flowed along the side of the hill until almost disappearing as it united with the river. So, I say, one might call this a natural armpit as it's almost invisible till you're here."

"I see," Jack said loudly and in a matter of fact way, "no ghosts or demons after all, just natural phenomenon."

"Yeah, well that's pretty boring if you ask me," Rich whined. "I'd hoped for ghosts and demons; that would've been more exciting. I'm going to look for some more of the gold you talked about. That is exciting." Rich moved out of the cavern and through the roots.

When Rich exited the cave Beth stood outside of the totem poles waiting.

"There's no need to worry little lady, nothing to see but a big hole in the ground and a bunch of natural phenomenon."

Beth stared at Rich with suspicion.

"Really Beth, there's no ghosts, no demons, just a big boring hole in the ground with wind blowing through it. Go take a look,"

She peered into the entrance for a second, and then turned back to Rich.

"It's not what I can see that worries me Rich."

She then went to the edge of the level area in front of the cave and gazed out over Whisper.

"Well," Rich said as he walked past her, "I'm going to get some more gold before we go. You just go ahead and stand here worrying Beth, if it makes you feel better."

Everything was gray as Beth peered out over the deserted buildings. She felt alone and empty, almost as if she were one of the cabins scattered around Whisper. The air entered her lungs heavy with moisture and a haze sat over the abandoned village. She shivered a little as the silent town seemed to be watching her, rather than her looking at it.

She examined the trails closely and slowly began to realize they all led to where she stood. She then noticed that the buildings appeared to be woven into the various trails. They were small at the outer edge but then became larger and more distinguished as their proximity moved closer to the cave.

Her mind struggled with this and she began to see something that frightened her; the entire layout of Whisper seemed to be a giant funnel; or...trap. She wanted to show this to Drew as soon as possible. The cold, or maybe this thought, caused her to tremble.

We should leave here soon Beth thought as she examined the strange configuration of Whisper. The woman at the trading post said only a few weeks remained before snow might move in on them. The five of them have been on the river now almost two weeks.

Jack had commented at one time that should it snow they would just stay on the river until reaching Jackson Point. This didn't really comfort Beth though. The thought of being in the kayak for an extended period, as snow fell on her and the others seemed desperate at best.

Inside the cave Cindy had become transfixed by one of the artifacts on the wall. Drew began investigating the hole again and though he had just established the reason for the sounds, he still struggled with

66

the assessment as he could almost hear words coming from the opening.

As his head turned different directions, the words would almost become clear. He turned his head this way a little and then another as someone might turn a knob while trying to tune a radio station in. Different voices would be heard as his head moved into different directions. One phrase seemed to be clearer than anything else.

"Don't leave us... Stay here... Don't leave us...Stay here."

To hear the sounds better he got down on his knees and leaned slightly over the hole, slowly turning his head in various directions. As he did this he began to make out more words and phrases. This shocked him. He couldn't believe a natural phenomenon would produce such sounds.

"Join us Drew...Don't leave us Dre..."

At the same time, behind Drew, Jack stepped behind Cindy and examined the artifact she had become so fascinated with.

"I want this for a souvenir." She suddenly said.

Reaching up she took hold of the middle and pulled, but the artifact had been anchored well to the wall.

"Just get one of those from the floor," Jack replied.

"No, this one still has color and look at the little skull in the middle, what is that?"

"I have no idea," Jack said and tilted his bottle up for another drink.

Cindy prodded all around the artifact, trying to get an idea of what held it to the wall. She then pulled again but it wouldn't come loose.

"Can you get this off for me?" she asked, turning to Jack.

Jack's face indicated he would rather not. But, after making a grunting sound he put the cork in the bottle and sat it down on the floor of the cave.

As he did this, Drew, still listening to the eerie sounds from the hole, noticed something shining directly opposite of him and protruding from the wall of the hole. He stared at it curiously.

Behind him, Jack reached up and grabbed the artifact Cindy desired. He pulled but it only gave a little.

Curious about the object Drew leaned forward a little towards it. He now determined it must be a very large nugget of gold embedded in the side of the opening.

Jack pulled hard on the artifact. Unexpectedly, it came lose and Jack fell backwards into Drew, causing him to fall straight into the opening, screaming as the darkness swallowed him.

Then, almost before anyone could grasp what had happened, silence permeated the interior of the cave.

Cindy screamed when she realized what had just happened.

Beth heard the scream and moved quickly to the cave entrance; stopping just before passing the totem poles.

"What's going on?" she yelled into the cave.

Jack tossed the artifact onto the floor and then leaned over the hole. "Drew! Drew!" he yelled into the pit.

"What's going on?" Beth now screamed into the cave.

Cindy came running out with tears streaming down her face. She stumbled and fell to the ground outside the cave beside Beth.

"What happened, where's Drew?" Beth knelt down beside Cindy trying to get answers.

Rich jumped up from beside the stream after hearing the scream and began making his way up towards the cave.

Still sobbing, Cindy mumbled something to Beth, but she couldn't understand her.

"What...What's going on Cindy? Tell me."

Cindy continued to cry but then in something of a shout she said.

"Drew! Fell! Ho-oo-lle," as she continued to sob uncontrollably.

"What?" Beth yelled out. "No, nooo! Drew!" she looked into the cave and screamed.

"Drew!"

Jack stared down into the darkness.

"Drew!" he yelled again and then listened. The whispering sounds had stopped completely and only the eerie silence came from the darkness of the hole.

Rich ran up to Cindy and Beth who were now both crying.

"What's going on?"

Neither of the girls could talk.

He ran into the cave where Jack still leaned over the opening.

"Where's Drew?" Rich asked trying to catch his breath.

Jack now sat back from his leaning position and looked very pale and exhausted.

"Where's Drew?" Rich asked again even louder.

"He. He. He fell in Rich." Jack replied with a weak voice.

"What?" Rich leaned down to the hole and yelled, "Dreeeeewwwwwwwwwwww!"

Jack got to his feet and stumbled towards the exit of the cave.

Cindy stood up, with her hand over her mouth and still crying she began moving towards the campsite just as Jack came out of the cave.

"What happened to Drew, Jack? Where is he?" Beth shouted at Jack as he appeared from behind the roots at the cave entrance.

"Drew fell into the hole." Jack sounded tired and he no longer appeared confident.

"We've got to go into the hole and look for him," shouting through her violent sobs.

Rich now came out of the cave with an expression of shock and confusion on his face.

"Rich, go get a rope, someone has to go look for him; he's probably hurt." Beth said, half shouting and half crying.

"Okay," Rich said and ran towards the campsite.

"It's too late Beth." Jack still sounded tired as he sat down on the ground.

"It's not too late!" Beth shouted as she turned and looked at Jack.

Then she froze in place. She stared at Jack for a few seconds as tears rolled down her face. Jack looked back at her and appeared to wonder why she had the strange look. Beth began to speak in a slow, strained voice.

"We don't have a rope... do we Jack?" Seething through clenched teeth as her tears momentarily dried. Jack suddenly recalled what Beth spoke of, sharply inhaling before exhaling very slow. He said nothing, but looked down at the ground at his feet.

"We don't have a rope, because you threw it out, so you could bring your booze, didn't you?" Beth exhibited obvious wrath. Jack still said nothing.

Beth turned away from Jack and thought for a few seconds. She put her face into the palm of her hands and then she wiped the tears that were close to falling from her eyes. Taking a deep breath she ran her fingers through her hair pulling it back from her face.

"Jack, we've got to find a rope. You or Rich have to go down and find him." She turned back around and looked at Jack who still sat with his arms draped over his knees staring at the ground between his feet. He turned his face to Beth.

"Beth, it's too late, I'm telling you. If you don't believe me, go look for yourself."

"I'm not going in there!" she yelled defiantly and again with anger in her voice. "I told Drew we shouldn't go in and he wasn't going to, but you guys had to drag him in. I'm going to find a rope and if you don't go in that hole, I'll bet Rich will. We're not going to just give up on him." Beth turned and walked briskly towards the large cabin that had the store goods and whiskey.

As she approached the large building she could see Cindy sitting at the campsite with her face in both hands, still obviously upset. Rich continued to search in vain for the rope. Beth reached the cabin and grabbed the wooden handle of the door, quickly pushing it open and taking several steps inside.

As her eyes focused in the dim light, her heart seemed to skip a beat. Fear grabbed her body and she immediately felt nauseous as the sight she beheld sent a shock through her entire body.

At the table where Jack, Cindy and Rich had been drinking the whiskey, sat the two Varga brothers. They didn't appear to be ghosts, but seemed real. The buttons on their shirts could be counted. Even the gray whiskers mixed in with the charcoal black ones strangely stood out in a sight Beth struggled to grasp.

She tried to move or scream; anything, but she'd become frozen with fear. As she stared at them her body began to shake without control. She labored to breathe the heavy air around her. One of the brothers looked up at her just as the scream she'd been straining to get out finally erupted from her lungs.

Beth stumbled backwards out the door as her mouth expelled the cry of terror. Falling to the ground she crawled on her hands and knees in an effort to get away from the cabin. Struggling, she stumbled to her feet and ran; in a mechanical fashion. Her heavy breathing rapidly formed mist in the cold air.

Staggering across the stream to a large rock Beth fell against it. She looked back through eyes filled with tears, expecting to see the two brothers behind her. Then, after feeling assured they hadn't followed her, she cried wearily and laid on the large rock, arms draped around it, holding the solid object in desperation for some form of safety.

CHAPTER SIX: THE FORSAKEN

"What's wrong?" Jack was the first to reach Beth. She couldn't talk though, or she didn't want to; she wanted to crawl under the large rock and find a safe place.

"What's going on?" Cindy now came running after hearing Beth scream. Rich soon followed asking about Beth.

"I don't know," Jack said to the others, "she won't say anything."

Cindy put her hand on Beth's back. "Are you all right Beth? What happened?"

Beth turned around and slid down the rock to a sitting position with her back against it. Her body was still shaking with fear.

"They're in the cabin," she replied, staring at the structure across the stream.

"Who's in the cabin?" Cindy asked.

"The Varga brothers were sitting in the cabin at the table when I opened the door." Beth's voice cracked through the tears.

"Who?" Cindy turned to Jack and he shrugged his shoulders?

"There's someone else around here?" Rich asked and looked around in dismay.

Cindy now squatted down beside Beth. "Beth who are you talking about? Are you all right?"

"They're in the cabin, they're here, all of them, they're still here; don't you understand?" Beth put her arms over her knees and laid her face in her arms.

"There's somebody in the cabin?" Rich asked, still appearing to be completely in the dark on the matter.

"I don't know," Cindy replied as she stood back up. "She's really upset, but she said she saw someone in the cabin."

"Come on Jack, let's go check it out!" Rich sounded eager to face the unseen trouble. The two started walking towards the cabin. Rich stopped, looking back at Beth and Cindy.

"I'll stay with her, you guys try to be careful."

Rich nodded and jogged a little to catch up to Jack.

As the two hopped across the rock area of the stream the whispering sounds began again. Jack stopped, holding his arm out to indicate to Rich he would be doing so. Turning his head slightly Jack noticed something different about the sounds.

"Listen."

Rich's face contorted a little as he tried to hear what Jack spoke of.

"The sound is different," Jack said. "You hear it?"

"Yeah its lower isn't it? Why do you think it sounds different?"

Jack gazed back at Rich and after a thoughtful second or two his face seemed to drop a little with sadness.

"It must be...Drew's body, lodged somehow in the cave and causing a different sound now. That's the only thing I know of that it might be."

Rich appeared a little shocked and disturbed by Jack's statement, but he nodded his head in confirmation that it must be the case.

As they continued on towards the cabin Rich searched the ground until he found a branch and broke it down to about the size of a police nightstick. The door of the lodge stood half open.

The two men moved slowly up to the door, trying to see inside before entering. After a few seconds of this, Rich moved inside first with his stick up in the air prepared to fight. After he'd moved inside, Jack stepped in behind him. They moved to separate sides of the door so the light from outside would come in.

Once they'd carefully examined the interior, they could see no signs of anyone having been there. The glasses they used earlier still sat on the table just as they had left them.

The two men strolled around the large cabin, inspecting it entirely before becoming relaxed again.

"What do you think?" Rich asked as he put his stick down. Jack moved around behind the counter and pulled another bottle of whiskey from the shelf.

"I think Beth may be having a breakdown," he then pried open the bottle. With the bottle in hand Jack went back around to the table and filled two glasses. Rich came over and the two sat down in the same chairs Beth had seen the Varga brothers sitting in.

After about ten minutes Cindy came to the door and peeked in. Jack looked at her as she stood in the door. Though Cindy was unaware of it, a strange re-enactment of what Beth had seen earlier occurred as Rich looked up, exactly as one of the Varga brothers had done.

"Well," Cindy stood at the door seeming to wait for the OK.

"There's no one in here," Jack said before taking another drink. "Beth may be falling apart on us." After swallowing the drink, he put the small glass on the table.

Cindy came in and sat at the table, Jack poured her a drink. She turned the glass up and then choked a little after swallowing the entire contents. Jack poured her another one. Rich took a drink also.

"I can't believe how bad things have gotten." She lowered her head and began to cry a little. Then she appeared to buffer up as she wiped a tear from her eye. "First Drew, now Beth is seeing things."

"How is Beth?" Rich asked.

"She's all right I guess, under the circumstances. She's just sitting there, on that rock, not saying anything."

"Do you really think she's losing it?" Rich asked and then took another drink and grabbed the bottle to refill the small glass.

Cindy turned to Jack. Jack sat back in his chair and peered into his tiny shot glass for a few seconds. He then turned to Rich and Cindy who were both looking at him as if waiting for an answer.

"I think she's just really stressed out about Drew," he took another drink as if to add emphasis to his statement. Rich and Cindy both took a drink as well in a gesture of agreement.

"Well, someone needs to go talk to her, she won't talk to me." Cindy pushed a strand of hair from her face and moved it behind her ear, then poured a little more in her small glass, seeming to welcome the effects of the alcohol.

"Yeah, we need to be getting down river before the snow comes, right Jack?" Rich asked Jack who remained reclining in his chair, cradling his glass with both hands. After a moment of thought Jack spoke.

"If you two will get everything packed up and ready, I'll talk to Beth."

Cindy and Rich agreed to this; then moved out of the large cabin and down towards the campsite.

As they moved down the hill they could see Beth sitting on the large rock with her arms crossed over her knees and her head lying on her arms.

Everything had become so much darker than when they started the trip. Everything looked gray now; gray and cold. Everything stood still. Beth didn't know the time of day and she didn't really care. She felt hungry though she didn't think she could eat anything if she did have something.

The whispering sounds became louder but sounded different from what she had heard before Drew fell into the hole. She tried to ignore them but somehow they found a way into her ears and the words she heard beckoned her to go to the cave and seek Drew. Jack walked up to her slowly so he wouldn't startle her. He thought she might be asleep so he spoke in a quiet voice.

"We checked the cabin Beth. If anyone was in there they must have slipped out or something. We couldn't find anyone."

She glanced up at Jack, but then put her head back down.

"Cindy and Rich are packing the stuff and getting the kayaks ready. We should leave soon. There's nothing else we can do for Drew and I think the stress is wearing you down."

Beth heard Jack but she didn't really want to look up again. After a few seconds however, she did look up at him. Her eyes were swollen and wet from crying. Jack spoke softly now.

"We need to leave Beth."

She turned her head and gazed out over Whisper. She appeared to be considering what Jack had said. After a moment she finally spoke with a broken voice.

"Do you really think it's going to be that easy Jack?"

He looked at Beth but she continued to gaze out over the ghost town. Realizing she wouldn't address him he looked down at the ground and then turned away from her.

"Look Beth, I'm really sorry about what happened to Drew, we all are. There was nothing we could do for him. Even if we had a rope, we couldn't have helped him." Turning around Jack met Beth's eyes straight on. She stared at him with a look of contempt.

"Is that what 'they're' telling you Jack? Is that what you hear while you drink their booze and sit in their cabin?"

The way Beth stared into his eyes made him feel uncomfortable. Now he felt his confidence begin to slip away. He struggled to regain his composure and wished he'd brought his bottle.

"They, who are they Beth," he replied gruffly.

He moved around in front of her and nervously started to pace. She followed him, never turning her eyes away.

"Beth, you're the only one that seems to believe there's someone else around here other than us. So tell me, why do you see these other people, or ghosts, or whatever it is when no one else does?"

She didn't seem shaken by Jack's louder voice and exaggerated movements. She thought about his question for a moment before replying. Jack, feeling he had her in a corner stood in front of her now waiting for an answer.

Then, in a monotone voice, Beth looked back over Whisper and softly replied,

"Maybe, I'm the only one that understands when to be afraid." She paused for a second.

"Or maybe, no one else can see them for the same reason a fish doesn't see the hook." Then Beth laid her head back on her arms, indicating she had no more to say.

Jack tried to think of a witty remark to her answer, but couldn't think of anything.

He stood frozen in front of her for a few seconds; her frightening statement almost taking hold of him. He quickly ran his fingers through his hair and slowly shook his head in disbelief that he would even consider such notions.

In frustration he made a grunting sound and marched down the trail towards the campsite.

Rich and Cindy had everything ready to go and sat around the remnants of the campfire, somberly gazing into it as if the dead blaze could still give them some form of comfort. Cindy turned to Jack with surprise.

"Where's Beth?"

"She's still sitting on that rock," He replied gruffly and sat down beside her. "I think she must be waiting for me or Rich to find a rope and go down in the hole looking for Drew."

"You want me to search the other cabins for a rope?" Rich asked, seeming eager to do anything other than sit.

"No, I told her it was to late for that. Even if we could find a rope what good would it do after sitting around for so long? The way she talks I think she's kind of lost it."

With that remark Rich blurted out. "You really think she's gone crazy?"

Jack glanced over at him and thought for a few seconds. Cindy now turned to Jack as if she also wondered about Beth's sanity. Jack replied with an apparent effort to sound confident and sure of his leadership abilities.

"She's determined to stick with the ghost thing, or whatever it supposedly was in the cabin. I tried to tell her what happened to Drew was a tragedy and we're all upset about it. But she insists that we just can't see these ghosts or whatever they are that she sees. It is like she doesn't want to accept the reality of the situation. She would rather sit on that rock and believe there's still hope for Drew, than accept the accident for what it was."

Jack now paused and gathered his thoughts again before continuing.

"I'm not for certain she's gone crazy, but she appears to be very close."

They sat silently, again staring at the dead campfire for a while. All three dwelt in their own thoughts of the loss of Drew and the complete turn of events.

Cindy put her head down as she would cry some and then she would wipe her eyes quickly and gaze out into the trees.

Rich stared at the ground and then at the dead fire. He wanted to go to the cave and look for Drew. But he felt Jack knew best, so he remained there.

Time seemed to stand still as they sat at the cold campsite. Now the feeling of being so far from home began to settle upon them.

Until recently they'd been confident and sure of themselves. But now as they sat in this vast wilderness alone, all three wanted to find people and not be alone anymore.

Finally, after the cold and moisture in the air began to soak in, Jack suggested they go back up to the large cabin. As they walked into the cabin Beth could be seen across the creek still sitting on the rock with her head on her arms. The hood of her jacket was pulled over her head and she appeared to be asleep.

Jack went straight to the table where a half bottle of whiskey sat along with the three glasses they had used earlier. After sitting down and pouring a small drink, Cindy got up and walked over to the door. Looking over to where Beth sat she said, "I'll go talk to her." She finished her drink, sat the small glass on the table and went out the door.

"Beth, you awake?"

Beth raised her head. She appeared to have either been sleeping or just exhausted. Her face and messy hair expressed the effects of the recent tragedy. She stared at Cindy wearily.

Cindy tried to cheer her up some with a little smile. Beth smiled the sad smile Drew had become so fond of.

Reaching into her coat pocket Cindy pulled out a granola bar and handed it to Beth.

"Thanks," she said and began opening the package. Cindy tried to think of something to say.

"Beth, I know you need to morn Drew, we all do. But we've got to leave here; we all realize it's not safe."

Beth chewed a bite of the bar not seeming to paying much attention to Cindy.

After eating the bite she turned to Cindy.

"Do you wonder why I'm the only one that hasn't given up on Drew?"

Cindy turned her head a little and didn't appear to understand what she meant.

Beth continued. "Don't you think it's a bit strange that they wouldn't let me look for a rope but they'll let you, Jack and Rich sit in their cabin and drink their whiskey?"

Cindy grimaced a bit. The statement from Beth frightened her. Yet she still wondered about Beth's mental state. She also considered herself stronger than Beth.

A part of her wanted to hug Beth and listen to everything she had to say. But another part considered Beth as unfit for the challenge they now found themselves in. She became determined to not allow Beth any control over her emotions.

"Beth, you're not thinking clearly. The stress has you all disoriented. What happened to Drew was a terrible accident and we're all saddened by it. But you've got to stop thinking all these crazy things."

Beth took another bite of the granola bar and chewed on it as Cindy talked.

After swallowing again and taking a pause to gather her thoughts she spoke in a soft tone.

"It wasn't an accident Cindy."

Now Cindy became more animated and began moving around much like Jack had done earlier.

"What do you mean it wasn't an accident? I was there. What are you thinking Beth? Are you trying to blame it on Jack?" Cindy's voice now grew louder.

"Listen Beth, you've got this all wrong if you're trying to blame Jack, it was just a horrible accident."

Beth watched Cindy as she paced back and forth and began speaking louder.

"In fact, I was the one that asked Jack to pull that stupid thing off the wall. You know, thinking about it now, I don't know why I wanted that thing to begin with. Jack didn't mean to fall into Drew, that, ridiculous thing on the wall just came loose all of a sudden." She waved her arm indicating the unexpected event.

"I asked Jack to pull it off the wall of the cave for me. So are you going to blame me as well?"

She stared at Cindy with a renewed interest in after hearing this.

"I wish I'd never asked Jack to pull that thing off the wall for me. But no one could have predicted such a thing Beth."

Cindy looked at Beth as if to receive confirmation from her. Beth simply stared at her without emotion and then slowly took another bite of her bar.

After realizing Beth wasn't going to comment Cindy continued as if she were pleading her case to a judge.

"Beth, no matter whether we had a rope or not it wouldn't have helped Drew. You should go look at that hole and then you'd understand."

Beth appeared to consider all that Cindy had said. Then without showing any emotion she finally spoke.

"You're wrong Cindy. I knew something bad would happen. And Drew would have stayed outside the cave with me if Rich hadn't pushed him in.

"I'm not crazy either. You, Jack and Rich don't see them because you're not struggling against them and this place. Right before Drew fell into the hole I realized something about Whisper. The way it's laid out. It's a trap Cindy; one great big methodical trap, and we're right in the center of it."

Cindy now had an expression of being frightened but she also seemed confused and bewildered by what Beth was telling her. Noticing that Cindy didn't understand, Beth continued.

"I don't think they want us to leave here, and as long as we don't struggle against them or try to leave they won't show themselves.

"You may think I'm just sitting here sulking Cindy, but I've been thinking about this place. I realize there may be no hope for Drew, but I also believe they're trying to manipulate us, as well as what we think.

"I'm hoping the situation will calm down enough so that we might be able to leave. I'm trying to..." Beth stopped talking mid-sentence.

Glancing over Cindy's shoulder she could see one of the Varga brothers walk around the corner of the large cabin. There could be no mistaking the old clothes and the bushy black beard. He walked in front of the cabin and stood looking over at Beth and Cindy. She scrunched down a little in an effort to escape his gaze. Cindy stared at her, still waiting for Beth to finish her sentence.

"Trying to what Beth? Really Beth, you're acting very strange. It's no wonder the guys think you're losing it. I've tried to consider the extra stress you are under but you really are starting to sound like a crazy person."

Beth, still scrunching down, made no reply, but kept an eye on the Varga brother.

After Cindy stopped talking Beth spoke but in a very low voice.

"Cindy, I think I know what we have to do. But you must do exactly as I say."

While she spoke she could see the Varga brother walking slowly closer. He began examining the two girls as a hunter might watch prey.

"Go get Jack and Rich. You all three must walk slowly and quietly down to the campsite. Stay there without making any noise. They're watching me very closely right now. But I'll be there as soon as things calm down. Then we can try to leave. Do you understand?"

Cindy stared at Beth for a few seconds with obvious frustration. She then looked over her shoulder to see why Beth had been talking so quietly. Not seeing anything she turned back to Beth.

"Yeah, fine Beth, whatever you say. Just try to hurry, all right." She turned and walked towards the cabin as if slightly aggravated by the situation.

"Cindy," Beth still spoke in a low voice.

"What?" Cindy turned around, clearly irritated now.

"I understand about Jack bumping into Drew. I don't believe it was his fault or yours either."

Cindy seemed to calm down some now.

"Yeah, all right, just don't take too long up here, okay?"

As Cindy passed in front of where the Varga brother stood he disappeared from Beth's view.

Now Beth noticed the whispering sounds beginning to subside. She tucked her head down to her arms but this time kept enough room between the hood of her jacket and her arms to see out. She watched Cindy until she walked through the door of the large cabin.

Inside, Jack and Rich had all but finished off the half full bottle of whiskey and both had obvious signs of too much alcohol in their system. Rich laughed after Cindy walked through the door.

"You don't have her either do you? You want me to go hog tie her Jack?"

84

Jack chuckled a little and turned to Cindy, raising his eyebrows in a questioning manner. Cindy sat down and picked up the bottle. Examining the remainder of the contents she realized how much the two had drunk since she left them.

"You two won't be able to operate a kayak when we do get her to move from that rock." She then poured the last bit of whiskey into a glass and drank it down.

"So, is she coming or not?" Jack asked.

She sat the glass on the table and seemed to try and catch her breath after the dose of whiskey.

"She said, we're to go down to the campsite, quietly, and wait there. As soon as the 'ghosts' or whatever it is she keeps seeing settle a bit, she'll come down and we can leave."

Jack immediately grimaced as if he had just eaten something very bitter. He staggered a little but managed to stand up. He took the bottle off the table and tipped it up to take a drink. When he realized he had an empty bottle he threw it violently across the cabin and it smashed loudly against the wall.

"So, the crazy one thinks she's running the show now?"

Rich, feeling uncomfortable about the situation took the opportunity to excuse himself.

"Well, whatever you guys decide on let me know; I'll just go down to the campsite and wait." He sidestepped Jack and moved out the door.

Cindy never budged from her seat and didn't appear to be frightened by Jack's actions.

"What's the difference, as long as we can get back on the river?"

Jack stared at Cindy almost as if she'd spoken foul language to him. He said nothing but walked behind the counter and took another bottle from under it. After prying it open he turned the bottle up and Cindy watched as air bubbles gave indication of a large drink.

"You're drinking too much," she said after he pulled the bottle down from his mouth.

"You and Rich are both way too drunk; you need to put the bottle away for a while."

His face became strained and it seemed he wanted to say something but held back. He stared at Cindy. She'd never seen him this way before. It must be the whiskey she thought to herself and turned away from his stare.

Jack moved back to the table and sat down. He poured Cindy a drink.

"I don't want anymore right now." She stood up and watched Jack lean back in the chair holding the whiskey bottle up to his chest as if it were a baby.

"You shouldn't be so hard on Beth. She realizes it was an accident. She knows you didn't fall into Drew on purpose."

When Cindy said this Jack appeared to start swelling up. His face became contorted and red with anger. He staggered out of his chair to face Cindy.

"You told her about that?" Jack appeared enraged.

Cindy appeared confused. "Well, yeah, she talked like she already knew about it. I thought you'd already told her."

Jack paced around in front of Cindy as if something were boiling inside him and trying to get out. Then he suddenly stopped in front of her.

"You stupid BITC-!"

Cindy heard nothing after those words, and barely saw the back of Jack's hand before it connected with her face. Everything went black.

When she could see again, Cindy found herself on the floor face down. Jack staggered around speaking loud and foully about her. She couldn't catch all the words as her head seemed to be swimming.

The side of her face that Jack slapped began to hurt and throb now. As she strove to get to her hands and knees, blood dripped from her mouth and landed on the rough floor in front of her.

Though the whiskey had made her feel warm and fuzzy before, it now fogged her mind and she couldn't think straight. She began to remember what happened but still felt lost and couldn't recall where she was or why Jack had hit her. She struggled in an attempt to get back onto her feet.

Jack paced back and forth almost screaming about something. Her ears were ringing. Cindy tried focusing. She began to feel afraid of Jack and this had never happened before. Managing to stand back up, she stumbled out the door past him as he turned the bottle up again.

Once outside, she fell to the ground. Getting back up and looking around she saw the campsite below and vaguely remembered it. She stumbled down the path towards it. Blood from her mouth and nose ran onto her jacket. She put her hand up to her face to stop the bleeding.

Beth had dozed off from sheer exhaustion. She awoke to loud shouts from across the stream and inside the cabin. Looking through the area between her arms and the hood of the jacket she saw Cindy stumble out the door and fall to the ground. The whispering sounds grew louder. She sat up.

Cindy got back to her feet and stumbled down the trail towards the campsite. Beth slid down from the large rock. Glancing to the cabin, Jack could still be heard yelling.

She turned towards Cindy again and now saw Rich moving up the trail towards her. He stopped and attempted to talk to her but she pushed him away. Rich then headed up the trail towards the cabin.

Beth watched closely as Rich peeked into the old building before going in.

"Jack, you in here?"

"What do you want?" The voice came from a corner to the right of him. Rich walked cautiously into the cabin to where Jack sat holding the bottle of whiskey.

"What happened to Cindy?" he asked meekly.

"None of your business is what happened." Jack still had anger in his voice. He appeared tired and intoxicated. Rich still felt the effects of the liquor himself, so he pulled one of the old rough chairs over to sit across from Jack.

"I know it is none of my business Jack, but maybe I could just sit here with you?"

Jack looked at Rich and took another small drink from the bottle.

"I've got a career waiting for me Rich; or at least I did have. That stupid woman is blurting everything to Beth, who I suspect is crazy." Jack's words were coming out slurred and his eyes were glazed.

"That crazy woman is going to tell everyone it's my fault Drew fell into that hole. She's going to ruin me Rich." Jack became animated as he spoke, sitting up and throwing his arm in the air. "She's going to ruin me, you understand? And Cindy is helping her. She should be on my side." Jack then leaned back into his chair and the shadows of the old room.

Cindy stumbled into the campsite. All the gear had been packed into the kayaks. She stood for a moment trying to regain her thoughts. Her face throbbed. Everything began to come back to her. She began to cry again. She started walking quickly towards the kayaks. She wouldn't stay anywhere that Jack was, ever again.

When she reached the kayaks she struggled to pull one lose. She realized they had all been tied together. This caused her to cry even more as she fought with the rope.

She went to the tree stump and pulled the tie securing the kayaks from it, releasing the one she wanted but also releasing the other two. She cared nothing about this or anything else. She wanted to get away, far away and as fast as she could.

Cindy climbed into the kayak and pushed into the deeper part of the lagoon and turned around. She paddled quickly down the stream and as she went under the trees and reached the river she began to cry again without control.

Nothing like this had ever happen to her. The river began to carry her. She would let it carry her where she needed to go. Jack had said all they needed to do was follow the river.

Cindy put her head down in her hands and cried hard and long. As she cried the kayak floated to the left and soon went down a branch of the main river. While she wept the current carried her swiftly into the vast Alaskan wilderness.

She began to look around as she wiped her eyes to clear them. Jack had said the river would take them to Jackson Point. She started to paddle as the realization of being totally alone begun to sink in. She was unaware that she moved farther and farther away from civilization. She had walked away at the trading post, before hearing the critical instructions of staying to the right of the river.

She became hopelessly lost in the Alaskan wilderness after leaving Whisper. As panic gripped Cindy, she continued to move the kayak faster in desperation. She slipped steadily into the vast expanses, where no human ear would hear her desperate cries for help. Cindy would never be seen again.

Beth watched the door of the cabin intently; she hoped Rich would come out and tell her what was going on. She soon realized after watching the door without any sign of Rich this wouldn't happen, she decided to check on Cindy. She moved slowly from the large rock that had given her the small fragment of security. After she got a few yards away her pace quickened. At the campsite nothing remained. She jogged nervously towards the small lagoon; calling out for Cindy.

Jack calmed down some but still showed signs of having drank too much. Rich began drinking again during their conversation. Both were almost too drunk to stand up when Beth ran up to the large cabin.

"The kayaks are gone! What did you do to Cindy, Jack?"

After scanning the inside of the large cabin cautiously, she walked straight up to Jack, staring at him with anger in her eyes.

Jack waved his hand and made a "ppt hh tt" sound with his mouth as if he didn't care what had happened to her.

"What did he do to Cindy, Rich?"

Rich expressed reluctance to say anything in front of Jack. Beth grabbed his arm and pulled him from his chair. He fell to the floor but then got back to his feet and followed her. Jack uttered some profanities towards Beth but she paid no attention.

"What did he do to Cindy, Rich? Tell me now!"

Now that they were away from Jack, Rich seemed more cooperative.

"I think he hit her, I tried to talk to her but she pushed me away. She was bleeding."

Beth grabbed him by the arms staring directly into his so he could see the fear radiating from her eyes in his drunken state.

"Rich, the kayaks are gone; do you understand what I'm saying?"

"Gone, what do you mean, gone? Why would she take all three?"

Beth thought about this for a second.

"No, she wouldn't need to take all three," she said, somewhat thinking out loud.

Then Rich blurted out, "Maybe she took one but didn't tie the others back up, they were all tied together. If she did that they may have floated down the stream."

She looked at Rich in amazement that he remembered such a detail in his condition.

"You're right. I bet that is what happened. I'll go see if they are somewhere downstream." She quickly jogged off towards the little lagoon again. Rich followed behind at a fast staggering walk rather than a jog until reaching the campsite; he fell to the ground as if unable to follow any farther.

Jack lingered in the large cabin by himself. He started to feel alone and wished one of his friends would come back inside the cabin. As if on cue he heard someone calling his name. At first he ignored it. But the slightly familiar voice was persistent.

"Jack...help me Jack."

He staggered to his feet and walked to the door. Opening the door he scanned the area around the cabin; no one could be seen but the voice remained calling out to him.

Who is calling out my name? Stumbling out the door he looked towards the cave and could hear the voice more clear.

"Jack...Jack! Please help me."

He staggered up the trail towards the cave. As he approached the cave the voice sounded familiar.

"Jack! Help me Jack."

He moved closer to the cave entrance; gazing carefully into the entrance before he moved through the roots.

"Drew? Is that you buddy?" He moved closer to the hole. "Drew, is that you, are you hurt?"

Sitting alone at the campsite the whispering sounds began to make Rich feel lonely. After several failed attempts to get to his feet he finally managed to stand up and began moving towards the large cabin. Rich noticed the door was standing open. As he approached the door he cautiously gazed inside where Jack had been sitting.

"Jack?" He moved through the door and looked all around the inside. Sitting down at the table he ran his fingers through his hair as if trying to decide what to do next. He used the edge of the table as leverage and brought his body back to a standing position, though the room kept spinning. Once he was able to focus on the door and felt confident his feet could bear his weight he walked to the door, scanned out over the area seeing no signs of Jack or Beth. Deciding to go to the cave and see if Jack had went back, he grabbed the door and pulled it shut as he left.

Climbing up the path towards the cave Rich stopped several times to look out over Whisper in an attempt to spot Jack. The whispers now began to sound comforting to him. As he moved closer to the cave he felt less alone.

Rich came to the front of the cave. The subtle sounds fluttered around his ears and beckoned him to come inside. He hesitated and turned to look over Whisper one more time in the hope of spotting Jack.

Inside the cave Jack got down on his hands and knees. Setting the bottle of whisky down, he crawled over to the edge of the hole. "Drew is that you?" Jack heard the voice clearly now.

"Jack,help me."

He crawled closer to the edge peering into the dark hole.

"Drew, I'll help you buddy, hang on. I'll find a rope, or something."

The whispers swirled around Jack's head now.

"Jack…Jack! Please help us Jack."

He was confused.

"Us, who are you?" Jack asked, becoming nervous. The whispers continued and just as he began to back away a voice came from behind him.

"Jack."

He moved his leg and something tapped it; knocking the bottle of whiskey over. When he turned around to see who had called his name he saw someone standing before him. It looked like Drew, but how could Drew be standing in front of him when the sound, his name, was called from someone behind him.

"Jack..." Now his name was called again by someone behind him.

His heart began to pound in his chest; frightened and disoriented. He moved forward to get away but realized he'd moved too far as he started to fall into the hole.

Unable to calm himself within that split moment Jack realized all the residents of Whisper awaited him in the dark regions he was now slipping helplessly into. He tried to scream out, but before he could the whispers embraced him and then the darkness swallowed him completely.

Outside the cave, Rich called out for Jack several times. Feeling completely alone he stood at the entrance of the cave being comforted by the whispers. Cautiously moving through the roots he called out for Jack. a

"Jack, you in here?" A half full bottle of whiskey lay on the floor of the cave but no sign of Jack otherwise.

Rich sat in front of the hole. He picked up the whiskey bottle, pulled the cork out and took a drink. Just as the bottle came down he noticed something from the corner of his eye. He looked over to the wall opposite of the large hole. A large gold nugget jutted out of the earth. He studied the nugget in a trance like manner.

The more he studied the nugget the more he wanted to reach over and pull the shining piece of gold from the earth. Rich didn't notice the whispering sounds growing louder and swirling around him. His attention had become fixed on the nugget.

He moved closer to the hole and put his arm out to see if he could reach it. A few more inches and he could take hold of it; the largest nugget would be all his.

Beth came back to the campsite after searching in vain for the kayaks. She looked around for Rich. Realizing the tone of the whispering sounds had changed again, she called out nervously for him; her breath misting in the cold Alaskan air.

The temperature continued to drop. The gray sky became darker; silence and stillness surrounded her.

She yelled for Jack in desperation, but no response came. Only the whispers replied. The sounds were soft but filled with angst.

Fear began to take hold of her as she ran towards the cabins, stumbling several times on the steep loose earth of the trails.

She came to the front of the large cabin. Beth didn't want to open the door. She felt terror when she took hold of the handle; she quickly let go. She knew she couldn't open it, so she beat on the door instead, calling out for Rich and Jack. She backed away in a vain anticipation that one or both would soon open the door.

She knew what had happened the last time she opened the door and she refused to open it again. Instead she turned and gazed out over Whisper, in the hope of spotting one or both of them.

The desolate town mocked her now. She reluctantly moved higher on the trail towards the cave.

When she reached the level area in front of the entrance she again looked out over Whisper. She examined the entire area closely hoping to spot Rich or Jack. She then turned and gazed at the ominous opening of the cave.

Approaching the totem poles she refused to cross the invisible line. She tried desperately to see in through the roots.

Inside the cave Rich felt the soil move slightly under his hand as he reached for the nugget. He almost had it, just a little bit…Nothing mattered to him except getting the large nugget. The whispers seemed to cheer him on now. He could almost hear the voices giving him encouragement.

"This treasure is for you Rich, just a little closer Rich."

His fingertip touched the nugget. A little bit more the voices seemed to say. He thought it had moved when his fingertip grazed it.

"Just a bit more Rich, move closer."

If he could just get a hold of it he was sure it would fall right into his hand.

He now extended all the way and moved one leg back to give him just enough counterweight to get the nugget. But then…

"Rich…!"

Outside the cave someone yelled for him.

"Rich…!"

It was Beth. Rich turned his head slightly in an attempt to answer her.

The soil of the cave gave way under his hand. He grunted and tried to catch himself. The whispers got louder and seemed to be laughing at him.

Rich gazed with terror into the darkness of the hole as he slid in. His mind raced as the voices beckoned him into the abyss. He screamed but it was too late. Whisper had him.

CHAPTER SEVEN: TEARS OF ABANDON

B eth heard something from inside the cave. She yelled inside again.

"Rich... Jack, are you in there?" No one replied.

The whispers began to grow louder; the sound of a multitude of voices moaning.

Beth stepped back, feeling completely panicked in the middle of an unseen force. She nervously turned around as a heavy snow shower fell from the sky at that instant, like a thick blanket coming down all at once.

Along the trails and around the cabins people were standing or walking slowly in her direction. All gazed upwards at her. She began to tremble without control.

She wanted to scream, but instinctively knew there was no one left to hear her; her friends were among the voices now.

She tried to walk but fell to the cold moist ground as her knees buckled from under her. Her heart beat so rapid she thought it would burst. Panic grasped her body and pulled her in all directions as she lay trembling uncontrollably on the hardened earth.

She didn't want to get up; she wanted to be swallowed by the earth and hidden from the voices swirling around her shaking body. Slightly picking her head up to peer at the trails and the cabins again, the legs of someone stood directly in her line of sight. Beth screamed, as her head jerked backwards, hitting the ground hard.

One of the Varga brothers stood gazing down upon her. She scrambled to get away from him but realized she was moving directly towards the entrance of the cave. She screamed, "No...!"

In a defiant effort she mustered all the courage she could and jumped up to her shaking feet. She began stumbling down the ravine as tears clouded her vision.

Everything became a blur. She didn't know where she was going. Along the paths Beth could see people staring at her with dark emotionless eyes. She knew they were the people of Whisper. All must have become victims of whatever it was in the hole of the cave; those having crossed the totem poles.

Running didn't seem to help; she couldn't get on the pathways as this is where the phantoms were. She scrambled through the short brush and stream dodging them.

Her heart still felt as though it were seconds away from bursting, but she was determined to not give up without a fight.

As she moved towards the outer part of Whisper, the ghosts had surrounded her in her efforts to leave the town behind. Frightened to the point of her body shutting down she continued to stumble from one side of the stream to the other in a frantic effort to avoid being trapped.

Every time Beth came upon a resident of Whisper she turned away and went to the other side trying to not look into their hollow eyes; to see the sunken, hollow faces. Yet even this was becoming harder to do as they closed in on her.

Soon she could see the boundary of the lost town; she endeavored to reach it and remain on course; fear pushing her forward. The phantoms were now virtually materializing in front of her. She screamed with fright and defiance.

"Nooo! No! Nooo!" she cried as she wiped her tear soaked eyes trying to see. Lowering her head she closed her eyes and bolted through them.

Only one thought raced through her mind. Get out of Whisper!

She moved to the right ascending the hill trying to keep in line with where she thought the river might be.

Beth pulled her hood farther over her head and looked down at the ground only peering out to stay on course.

Then, as she finally came to where the farthest path would be, she came up to a young girl. The girl looked directly into Beth's eyes but showed no emotion.

Dressed in a late nineteenth century dress with a laced apron the little girl held a handmade doll in one hand.

Beth broke at this point and began crying so hard she had trouble seeing through her tear flooded eyes. She moved around the young girl and ran without stopping. She stumbled and fell; got up and ran again, always trying to run towards the river.

The river would be her only hope. If she could follow the river maybe she could make it to civilization. She had too try. She wouldn't give in to them without a fight.

After what seemed to be miles of running she made it to the top of the ravine. Stopping at the top to catch her breath. She felt she had won a small victory; the crying had ceased. But then...

In the whispers she heard a familiar voice. Beth froze.

"Beth... Beth..." Frozen she listened to the once comforting voice.

"Drew?" She felt her strength leaving. "Please help me Drew." She said in a whisper.

"Beth," the voice said again. The flood gate once again opened and she sobbed as her hands took hold of her fallen head.

"Drew, I'm sorry... I'm sorry, but I can't go back, I can't." She fell down to her knees and continued to hold her face in her hands as she wept.

All the while the whispers beckoned her to the cave. She thought about giving up and going to the cave, to be with Drew and her friends. How would she ever get away from here? How would she ever make it out of the Alaskan wilderness alone?

The snow fell again like a thick, warm blanket. Darkness began to take hold of her as she could feel the courage leaving her body and hope evaporating from her soul.

As she contemplated giving up and giving into the darkness, something strange occurred, like a breeze changing direction; Drew's voice was now in front of her rather than from behind her.

She looked up. His voice now called out to her in the direction she had been running, rather than from Whisper.

Behind her the sounds from the cave became stronger as if struggling to keep a hold on her. The moaning melted together in unison. She turned back to the front, straining as if to see Drew's voice.

"Beth, hurry Beth." When she heard this she stood up, she wiped her eyes and began to walk towards the voice.

"Drew, where are you?" Feeling disoriented, she turned back to look at Whisper.

With the snow on the ground distinguishing the trails around the ghost town, Beth perceived a terrifying sight. The paths leading to the cave looked to be laid out as some type of massive spider web. The snow covering the grass and brush along both sides outlined the trails revealing distinctly what the others never noticed.

Beth now grasped with clarity what she had wanted to show Drew.

The cabins sat ominously along the paths and altogether the town presented the configuration of a massive trap.

As she stared at the cave she saw what looked to be two large rocks on the top part, where they were not noticeable close up. The snow on top of these caused the outline of the rocks to resemble two large eyes and the entrance of the cave from this distance seemed like a large open mouth. The two totem poles resembled large bottom teeth sticking up similar to that of a wild hog.

It all appeared as a strange creature buried in the hill with only the face visible, laying in wait for unsuspecting prey. The trails resembled a web that moved the victims closer to the huge mouth.

Once the people crossed the totems, perhaps a spell had been placed on them and they continued to return to the cave until finally falling into the pit to their doom.

With these thoughts and recalling the strength she had summoned earlier, Beth found a new sense of determination; turning again moving forward out of Whisper's sight.

She walked as fast as she could in the direction of the river and Drew's voice. The farther she moved from Whisper the better she felt. Soon, she could no longer hear Drew, but she continued in the direction he had led her thus far.

The damp cold and snow began to make its presence felt. Beth shivered-cold, hungry, and weak. She realized the only thing she had eaten for days had been snack bars; Cindy had given her one that morning.

Beth no longer could hear Drew, but the whispers continued to follow her as a predator might chase its prey.

Slowly they too became less and less noticeable. As her strength began to wane she vaguely spotted the river ahead.

Uncertain if once she reached the river what she was then going to do, she set her goal to simply reach the river.

As she approached the waterway and moved downhill Beth spotted something red. She tried to move faster and though her legs resisted every step she forced herself onward.

The red object slowly came into view and her spirits lifted that she began to laugh and cry as she now ran down the hill towards the river.

A large tree had fallen with most of it lying in the river; caught by this tree, was one of the kayaks. Beth kept her eyes on it as if the small craft would leave if she took her eyes off of it.

Just as she got close to the water she ran into something and fell face forward, tumbling over and over almost into the river.

When she stopped tumbling the pain in her lower right leg came immediately. Holding her leg and screaming out with pain she turned back to see what she had run into.

There on the hill, partially covered by moss and vegetation stood a pyramid structure very much like the one they had seen before finding Whisper.

Her body quivered from pain, exhaustion, and adrenaline as she attempted to make out the strange rock structure. Whisper is trying to capture her one last time, she thought.

Shaking her head as if this would take the pain of her leg away, the whispers disappear, and the strength to make it to the kayak, she made a slow, shaking effort to stand on her good leg. Beth made three attempts before finally standing up on her good leg. Taking a deep breath, Beth hopped painfully to the kayak. Struggling through the tears and excruciating pain she positioned herself into the craft and used the paddle to move out to the river. Pulling the paddle from its holder she attempted to get as far from Whisper as possible.

Beth faded in and out of consciousness as she floated down the waterway. She made every effort to stay awake as she feared of drifting into a branch that hung out over the river and floating off into the Alaskan wilderness, never to be found.

The snow fell hard on her and she pulled the hood over her head leaving only enough room to peek out from time to time, trying to make sure she always stayed to the right of the river. She lost all track of time as everything became hazy in her mind.

Then what seemed like hours had passed and all hope of reaching civilization had faded, Beth thought she heard the distant voice of a person. Her head had become almost fixed in a leaning position; struggling she lifted her head and peered out to where she heard the call.

There on the river bank stood several people waving their arms. She could barely see them through the heavy snow. She struggled to make her arms move. She put the paddle into the river and steered towards the river bank.

The people ran along beside the river to intercept her at the point she would hit the bank. Finally, she connected with land and two men in large heavy coats pulled the kayak onto the river bank.

As they helped her out of the kayak, Beth could only muster enough strength to whisper: "Help me, please." Then, as a long distance runner might collapse at the finish line, she fell into their arms and lost consciousness.

CHAPTER EIGHT: A TAINTED DELIVERANCE

B eth awoke in a Fairbanks hospital. "How long have I been here?" she asked weakly.

"You've been here almost two days Sweetie; in and out of consciousness most of that time," the nurse called for assistance on the intercom to alert the staff Beth was finally awake and speaking.

The nurse informed Beth that her lower right leg had been fractured, she suffered from mild hyperthermia, exhaustion, and was overly dehydrated. Beth was happy to be alive despite her physical injuries; they would heal over time.

A few days later an Alaska State police and a detective visited her. Beth told them everything she remembered from the time the group had started the trip, until she awoke in the hospital bed.

"Thank you Ms. Reynolds," the detective said. "I think I have what I need for now, but we may need to ask you some more questions later," the detective then closed his notebook. Beth nodded and the two men walked out of her hospital room and into the hall.

Once the two men were in the hallway the police officer looked at the detective and seeming rather bewildered said, "That's some story. I mean ghosts and whispering caves?" After a brief pause he continued.

"Do you really think they found Whisper?"

The detective thought about this for a second.

"Well, I don't know about the ghosts or the cave, but there are hundreds of old prospector cabins out in the woods where they were. They may have just found a few of these old cabins and buildings and thought it to be Whisper."

"Hmm," the police officer replied. "Yeah, you're probably right. Do you think she's crazy?"

The detective thumbed through his notes and didn't answer right away.

"I think, right now, we've got a bunch of college kids coming to Alaska and thinking they're going to have a two-week party on the river. Unfortunately, we've seen this type of thing before.

"I suspect they got in way over their heads and this girl is lucky to have made it out alive."

As the detective said this another officer walked up to them and pulled out a small notebook from his pocket.

"Hello Lieutenant Brooks," the detective said. The newly arrived Lieutenant greeted them.

"What brings you here?" The detective asked.

Lieutenant Brooks opened his notebook. "Well, I'm not sure what information you've obtained from Ms. Reynolds, but I've got what I believe is some interesting information here. We had no names to work with until Ms. Reynolds regained consciousness recently. But since then I've made some phone calls. I hoped I might catch you before you left. I would like to compare notes if you have the time."

The detective appeared interested and suggested the Lieutenant go on.

"First, when I spoke to the parents of Drew Martin, they indicated he was going on vacation with a girl he met at college." The Lieutenant stopped and looked at the other two men as if waiting for something.

After a few seconds the detective shrugged his shoulders indicating he didn't see anything abnormal about this information. So Lieutenant Brooks continued.

"I contacted the college Drew attends and there is no Beth Reynolds enrolled at his school."

The detective and police officer immediately perked up when they heard this.

"There's more," the Lieutenant continued. "I investigated the address Ms. Reynolds listed as her residence. It's a shelter for homeless women."

The detective and the officer looked at each other again with obvious surprise.

"Well, well, this is interesting information," the detective said, becoming much more attentive. "Is there anything else?"

"Yes, actually there is one other thing of interest. After contacting the shelter, I was able to track down Beth Reynolds' mother. I called her. Mrs. Reynolds immediately became somewhat hysterical and began crying uncontrollably when I told her why I was calling her. When she finally calmed down enough to talk, she explained to me that she had initially thought I'd called to tell her Beth was dead." Lieutenant Brooks paused momentarily.

Again the detective and police officer shifted their stature and presented an appearance of surprise. The Lieutenant continued.

"Her mother informed me that Beth's stepfather is an alcoholic and was abusive to Beth. I also got the suspicion Beth's mother struggles with alcohol.

"Anyway, Beth left home not long after she turned seventeen and her mother hasn't heard from her in over four years."

The detective took a deep breath as if trying to take all of this new information in. Then something seemed to come to him.

"What about a police record?"

"I thought the same thing so I checked. There's nothing at all; she has no criminal record, not even a parking ticket."

The detective pondered this for a few more seconds. The police officer who had listened to this information asked, "What do you think detective, foul play?"

The detective studied the police officer's question for a few seconds before answering.

"I believe we need to ask Ms. Reynolds a few more questions."

The officer and the Lieutenant both agreed and all three walked back into Beth's room.

Beth had already laid back down when the three men knocked on the door.

"Excuse me Ms. Reynolds," the detective said as he slowly opened the door.

Beth looked at the door as she began adjusting herself so she would be in more of a sitting position.

"We would like to ask you a few more questions, if it's all right with you."

"Yes, it's all right," she said.

The detective then introduced Lieutenant Brooks.

"It's nice to meet you Lieutenant," Beth replied.

"Ms. Reynolds, we have a few more questions to complete our picture we are trying to piece together before heading back to the office."

After the detective said this, Beth nodded in agreement.

"So, where did you and Drew Martin meet Ms. Reynolds?"

Beth now examined the three men with apprehension.

"We met at the college library," she finally said in a slow nervous voice.

The detective scribbled something in his notebook and then continued.

"And did you and Drew take some of the same classes together?"

Beth stared at the men with suspicion and seemed to be considering the question carefully. When she answered she again spoke slowly and almost in a whisper.

"We didn't go to class together, I don't attend the college." She lowered her head now and focused her attention on her hands.

"You don't go to the college, but you were at the college library?" The detective asked with a suspicious tone.

"Yes, that's right," she replied softly without raising her head.

"What were you doing in the library if you don't go to school there?" he asked, now staring at Beth intently.

"I just go there to read. It is close to where I live. I don't take anything; I just read the books in the library." Beth raised her head slowly and a bit defiantly. "Is there a law against that?"

"No, Ms. Reynolds, there's no law against that." The detective's tone more considerate than before. "But you must understand Ms. Reynolds this is a very unusual case."

She looked the detective straight in the eyes.

"I understand."

The detective stared into Beth's eyes as well, thinking she would back down if she had something to hide. Beth didn't back down and the detective turned away after a few seconds.

As this was taking place, the Lieutenant who had been standing behind the detective saw Beth's jacket hanging on a coat rack in the corner. Lifting it up he realized something caused the jacket to be much heavier than it should be.

"Is this your coat Ms. Reynolds?" the Lieutenant asked as he lifted it up and down indicating he knew something heavy was in the pockets.

"Yes, it is mine," She replied.

The Lieutenant handed the jacket to the detective. He also lifted the jacket up and down to get a feel for the weight.

"Do you mind if we check your coat?"

"No, I don't mind, go ahead." Beth answered, seeming a bit saddened by the nature of these new inquiries.

The detective opened a pocket and reached inside. He pulled out a hand full of gold nuggets, and then poured them onto the table beside Beth. This created a loud clanking sound as the heavy gold hit the table. The three men peered down at the precious metal for a few seconds. Beth also looked at it but expressed no emotion.

"What can you tell us about the gold Ms. Reynolds?"

"It is mine," she replied. "I gathered it from the side of a stream in Whisper."

"All of this gold was found at a stream?" The Lieutenant behind the detective moved around to ask.

"Yes, all of it," she replied quickly. The detective gathered the gold and poured the nuggets back into the pocket of the jacket.

"We'll need to hang on to this coat Ms. Reynolds, until we have a better understanding of everything involved in this case. No worries, you will get all your stuff back once we have more of these issues resolved."

Beth nodded that she understood, and the three men left noting how emotionless she was upon the discovery of the gold nuggets.

Later, she slept but not soundly. She found herself in Whisper; walking into the large cabin. Jack stood inside watching her with an expressionless face.

Everything moved slowly. Beth wanted to leave but every little movement required a large amount of effort. Rich stood behind the counter slowly pouring a drink. He looked up at her with hollow and distant eyes.

She looked around for Drew. She slowly examined the gray interior. Cindy sat in a darkened corner with her face in her hands. She was crying.

Beth became frightened. She turned to leave. The Varga brothers stood in the doorway. Behind them Drew called to her. She could see his hand reaching out to her.

"Beth. . .Beth."

She began to cry as she struggled to get to the door. Her body began to tremble.

"Drew, no... Drew...." She screamed as she held her hand out in an effort to reach him behind the Varga brothers.

"Drew! Drew!"

Nurses came into her room; quickly turning on the lights. Beth found herself sitting up in bed with her arm reaching out and tears streaming down her face.

The nurses tried to calm her down. As she lay back her entire body trembled without control, just as it did the day she left Whisper.

A nurse gave her a shot. As the medication took effect Beth fell asleep whispering.

"Drew...Drew..."

As the days went by, Doctors came and went in an effort to determine if Beth was insane; questions and silly tests filled each day in the hospital. No matter what test or how many different ways they asked the same question, she never changed her answers or her story.

The Doctors eventually determined she was quite sane. They each attempted to convince her that the things she saw at Whisper were contrived by an imagination under stress. Beth listened but said nothing more, realizing they would never believe her.

The detectives came and went almost every day for weeks, until they too determined she told the exact story she had the day they first questioned her. Others came and spoke with Beth. People related to the search party of her missing friends and those individuals of the Alaskan Natural and Forestry Services assisting with the search of the four young college kids.

Reporters came too. Beth became a spectacle as the search for the lost ensued. They asked her many questions but Beth had been advised not to say anything, for her own protection.

Since the reporters could get little from her, they often simply made stuff up. Beth watched the news painfully as opinions were given that described her as incompetent or heartless for leaving her friends in the Alaskan wilderness.

The extremely harsh winter caused sporadic and limited air travel in and out of Fairbanks. But the families of those lost at Whisper began arriving in search of answers.

Jack's family arrived first and before winter ever began to release its icy grasp on Fairbanks. As Beth lay in the hospital bed his parents questioned her over and over.

His mother eventually blaming Beth for their son's loss. She yelled angrily at Beth for leaving Jack and the others in the woods. As the nurses and Jack's father tried to pull her from the room she threw hate-filled curses at Beth.

She wept alone in her hospital bed until falling asleep from exhaustion.

Then Cindy's parents came and also blamed Beth for their daughter's loss. Beth lay staring silently at the wall as Cindy's parents shouted insinuations and accusations at her. A single tear trickled down her face as she could think of nothing to tell them.

The State of Alaska didn't want to lose track of Beth during the investigation, so after she was well enough to leave the hospital they sent her to a shelter for women.

Rich's parents came. They were obviously broken by the loss. Initially they tried to be compassionate towards her. Still, they had heard the stories by now from the other families and spoke with an underlying distrust of Beth.

The day finally arrived that she had dreaded. Drew's parents made their way slowly up the stairs to her room. His father initially seemed to distrust Beth. But she could no longer hold her feelings in.

Beth broke down in tears and told them how much she loved Drew and missed him. She cried on his mother's shoulder and emotions that had been suppressed were released in a torrent.

Drew's parents were the only ones that left Beth believing her to be innocent of any wrong.

Eventually, as the seasons slowly passed, all of the people stopped coming.

On a warm summer day, the detective returned to speak with Beth.

"Ms. Reynolds." The detective tapped on Beth's open door as she stood gazing out at the streets of downtown Fairbanks.

"Oh, hello Detective," Beth replied as she turned to him.

"Ms. Reynolds, I've come to tell you the State of Alaska will not be pressing any charges against you regarding your missing friends. And, I'm sure the search for them will continue in some capacity, but I'm afraid there's practically no hope they could have survived the harsh winter."

Beth made no comment. She had long ago given up hope of anyone else surviving Whisper. She nodded to the detective as she rubbed her arms together, as if feeling cold.

The detective continued.

"You're free to leave any time you wish. We're grateful for your cooperation."

The detective paused a second and felt a tinge of compassion now for this young woman who appeared to be completely lost in thought and emotions.

"Your belongings have been released. You can pick them up any time. Here is a receipt. Take this to the holding area to retrieve your things."

Beth took the small piece of paper and thanked the detective. He smiled a little and then left. She closed the door behind him.

Sitting on the bed she and tried to think of where to go. She tried to recall a time before Whisper. It was difficult to do. There seemed to be nothing before Whisper and Drew.

After putting a few pieces of donated clothing in a paper bag she went down the stairs.

Mrs. Roberts, the shelter caretaker looked up from her sweeping and noticed Beth walking down the stairway with the small bag in her hand.

"Now just where do you think you're off to Elizabeth?"

Beth smiled at her. Mrs. Roberts had a beaming nature that had kept Beth from hitting rock bottom on several occasions.

"The detective said I'm free to go now." She stepped down, level with Mrs. Roberts as she said this.

"Yes, but where are you going to go dear?"

Beth shook her head and gazed down at the floor.

"I don't know. I've got to go though. I'll go crazy if I don't."

"Do you even have a dollar to your name?"

She shook her head no again.

Mrs. Roberts glanced around to see if anyone else might be close by. When she spotted no one, she reached into her bra and pulled out a number of folded bills. She then pulled several twenty dollar bills from them and offered these to Beth.

"Here you are dear. I wish you would stay here a bit longer but I know you've been waiting to get away."

"No, Mrs. Roberts, I can't take that. Really, you'll need that money." Beth waved her hand as she said this.

"You can take it. Beth, you will take it. Don't go getting sassy with me young lady."

Beth smiled again when Mrs. Roberts said this. She then reluctantly took two twenty dollar bills out of the wad.

"Thanks Mrs. Roberts. I'll pay you back." As she said this Beth put the money in her pocket.

"You don't worry about that Elizabeth. You just take care of yourself." Mrs. Roberts then went back to her sweeping.

Beth gave her a quick hug and left through the front door.

She walked along the streets of Fairbanks in a daze. Several times she bumped into someone as her mind searched for anything to help her find a new place to start.

Then, passing by a store window and glancing up, she thought she saw Drew inside looking at a book.

Beth froze in front of the window. She stared at the man intently. Then he raised his head and she realized he merely looked like Drew from the distance. As her head lowered in disappointment, something familiar came into view.

There in a display was the most recent book by Candace Clarendon. The release date was no more than a week old. Beth looked at the store a little closer and realized she was standing in front of a bookstore.

Slowly she walked into the store. After a few moments Beth sat the new Candace Clarendon book, a writer's journal and some pens on the checkout counter.

The young man at the counter seemed to desire conversation with Beth. He took a look at the writer's journal before ringing it up.

"So, are you a writer?"

Beth smiled a little but didn't respond.

"I thought so. I can tell a writer when I see one. You've got that far away look; as if a great story is being spun inside your mind at this very moment." He then smiled a little as if trying to flirt.

Beth again smiled briefly and asked the young man.

"Can you tell me where the police station is? I seem to have become a little disoriented."

"Sure, you just go down this way about five blocks and you'll see it on your right."

Beth paid the young man and thanked him. She then went back outside. She pulled the book from the sack and examined it. Then she started walking towards the police station.

Eventually she came to the building and walked inside. She asked the person at the front desk for directions to retrieve her personal items.

After another short walk she arrived at a room with a counter and rows of shelves behind it. A lady in a police uniform greeted Beth.

"Can I help you?"

"I've come to pick up my things," Beth sat her bag on the counter and then handed the paper to the police woman. The woman took the small paper and examined it closely.

"Say, aren't you the girl they pulled out of the river about half frozen a while back."

"Yeah, I'm afraid that's me," Beth replied.

The Police woman pulled a file from a cabinet under the counter. After retrieving some papers from the file she walked towards the back of the room scanning them along the way. Soon she returned with Beth's jacket and laid it on the counter.

"You may want to check that everything is there. Once you leave here it's difficult to make a case for lost items." After saying this she examined Beth with interest for a few seconds.

"Did they ever find any of your friends?"

"No, they never did," Beth said with a sad tone.

"Oh, I'm so sorry to hear that."

"Yeah," Beth replied looking down as the memories returned to her. Then the lady turned and started towards the back. She walked in a different direction this time, again examining the papers as she went.

Beth reached into a pocket of the jacket and pulled a hand full of gold nuggets out. She gazed at them for a few seconds and then put them back. She then reached into another pocket and pulled out the small red antique snuff bottle Drew had bought for her at the trading post.

Immediately upon seeing the bottle, the whispers from the cave entered her ears. She quickly sat the bottle on the counter and rubbed her fingers on her blouse, as if she had touched something hot.

She gazed at the bottle as one might look at a scorpion or spider. Her transfixed stare only broke when the lady approached the counter carrying Beth's large denim bag.

The bag was obviously heavy and the lady labored as she carried it and then heaved it up to the counter.

"This is yours also, right?"

"Yes," Beth said, obviously happy to see the bag again. "I thought it was lost forever."

"What do you do Miss, collect rocks? That thing is heavy," the policewoman spoke with a bit of sarcasm.

As Beth looked over her bag the woman continued.

"You'll need to go to the motor pool holding area to collect your kayak and camping gear, we don't have room for such things here."

Beth opened the denim bag revealing the mass of gold nuggets Rich had filled it with.

"Wow," the police woman's eyes widened at the sight in the bag. "Is that what it looks like?"

Beth peered at the gold for a few seconds. Then she carefully placed the Candace Clarendon book and writers journal inside with the gold. She closed the bag back up.

Slowly and with some sadness in her voice Beth replied.

"That... is a promise." Then with some effort she put the bag across her shoulders and picked up the coat Drew had bought for her.

"A promise?" the woman asked, appearing puzzled.

Beth said nothing but turned to walk away.

"Hey Miss, you forgot your little bottle."

Beth turned back and took a step towards the bottle. She stopped. A painful expression came across her face and then she spoke softly.

"Can you throw it away for me please? I can't take it."

The police woman looked at the unique little bottle.

"Well, I suppose I can, but why don't you want it?"

Beth continued to stare at the tiny bottle; her face tightened even more, as if it were poison sitting on the counter. Her eyes squinted slightly.

"It came from Whisper," she finally said. "I can't take it; just get rid of it for me, please."

"Whisper?" the woman again appeared surprised and puzzled. "I thought that place was just a myth."

"No, it's not a myth," Beth replied.

"Well, all right," the woman said, "if you're sure about it."

Beth gave no reply but turned and left the police station, disappearing into the faceless population.

Oliver Phipps

A Subtle Yearning

Seventeen year's later in Fairbanks Alaska several young couples strolled into an outfitter shop.

After accumulating various items related to hiking and camping, one of the couples made their way to the counter.

The young woman then appeared to become spellbound by an item behind it.

Becoming aware of the woman's fascination, the young man that accompanied her asked the lady at the counter if they could see the item.

"Sure," she replied and taking the small item from the shelf, handed it to him. As he held the item in his hand the young lady with him stared at it and her eyes lit up.

Noticing she was very interested in it, the woman behind the counter began to elaborate.

"There's an interesting story about that little red bottle. My aunt gave it to me for a birthday present around, oh fifteen years ago maybe. She's a police woman downtown. According to her, a woman about your age was pulled from the river almost half dead.

"Some time later, after she recovered, she gave that little bottle to my aunt. The woman also told my Aunt, that particular bottle came from the lost gold town of 'Whisper.'"

The man looked at the young woman as she gazed with delight at the small bottle. He then turned to the woman behind the counter and asked.

"Would you sell it?"

The End

Oliver Phipps

We hope you enjoyed Tears of Abandon by Oliver Phipps. For your convenience we've listed some additional Oliver Phipps books below, which you may also enjoy. For a complete list of Oliver's books please check online or visit www.oliverphipps.com

THE HOUSE ON COOPER LANE

http://www.amazon.com/dp/B00JCFS9ZC

It's 1984 and all Bud Fisher wants to do is find a place to live in Madison Louisiana. With his dog Badger, they come across a beautiful old mansion that was converted into apartments.

Something should have felt odd when he found out nobody lived in any of the apartments. To make matters worse, the owner is reluctant to let him rent one. Eventually he negotiates an apartment in the historic old house, but soon finds out that he's not quite as alone as he thought. What ghostly secret has the owner failed to share?

It's up to Bud to unravel the mysteries of the upstairs apartments, but is he really ready to find out the truth?

A Tempest Soul

http://www.amazon.com/dp/B00MJDZQWI

Seventeen-year-old Gina Falcone has been alone for much of her life. Her father passed away while she was young. Her un-affectionate mother eventually leaves her to care for herself when she is only thirteen.

Though her epic journey begins by an almost deadly mistake, Gina will find many of her hearts desires in the most unlikely of places. The loss of everything is the catalyst that brings her to an unimagined level of accomplishment in her life.

Yet Gina, soon realizes it is the same events that brought her success that may also bring everything crashing down around her. The new life she has built soon beckons for something she left behind. Now, the new woman must find a way to dance through a life she could have never dreamed of.

WHERE THE STRANGERS LIVE

http://www.amazon.com/dp/B00TLNFQNS

When a passenger plane disappeared over the Indian Ocean in autumn 2013, a massive search gets underway.

A deep trolling, unmanned pod picks up faint readings and soon the deep sea submersible Oceana and her three crew members are four miles below the ocean surface in search of the black box from flight N340.

Nothing could have prepared the submersible crew for what they discover and what happens afterward. Ancient evils and other world creatures challenge the survival of the Oceana's crew. Mysteries of the past are revealed, but death hangs in the balance for Sophie, Troy and Eliot in this deep sea Science Fiction thriller.

Twelve Minutes till Midnight

http://www.amazon.com/dp/B00JSAM0RO

A man catches a ride on a dusty Louisiana road only to find out he's traveling with notorious outlaws Bonnie and Clyde.

The suspense is nonstop as confrontation settles in between a man determined to stand on truth and an outlaw determined to dislocate him from it.

"Twelve Minutes till Midnight will take you on an unforgettable ride."

DIVER CREED STATION

http://www.amazon.com/dp/B00LY58NWM

Wars, disease and a massive collapse of civilization have ravaged the human race of a hundred years in the future. Finally, in the late twenty-second century, mankind slowly begins to struggle back from the edge of extinction.

When a huge "virtual life" facility is restored from a hibernation type of storage and slowly brought back online, a new hope materializes.

Fragments of humanity begin to move into the remnants of Denver and the Virtua-Gauge facilities, which offer seven days of virtual leisure for seven days work in this new and growing social structure.

Most inhabitants of this new lifestyle begin to hate the real world and work for the seven day period inside the virtual pods. It's the variety of luxury role play inside the virtual zone that supply's the incentive needed to work hard for seven days in the real world.

In this new social structure, a man can work for seven days in a food dispersal unit and earn seven days as a twenty-first century software billionaire in the virtual zone. As time goes by and more of the virtual pods are brought back online life appears to be getting better.

Rizette and her husband Oray are young technicians that settle into their still new marriage as the virtual facilities expand and thrive.

Oray has recently attained the level of a Class A Diver and enjoys his job. The Divers are skilled technicians that perform critical repairs to the complex system, from inside the virtual zone.

Oliver Phipps

His title of Diver originates from often working in the secure "lower levels" of the system. These lower level areas are the dividing space between the real world and the world of the virtual zone. When the facility was built, the original designers intentionally placed this buffer zone in the programming to avoid threats from non-living virtual personnel.

As Oray becomes more experienced in his elite technical position as a Diver, he is approached by his virtual assistant and forced to make a difficult decision. Oray's decision triggers events that soon pull him and his wife Rizette into a deadly quest for survival.

The stage becomes a massive and complex maze of virtual world sequences as escape or entrapment hang on precious threads of information.

System ghosts from the distant past intermingle with mysterious factions that have thrown Oray and Rizette into a cyberspace trap with little hope for survival.

GHOSTS OF COMPANY K

http://www.amazon.com/dp/B00IE4QM7O

Tag along with young Bud Fisher during his daily adventures in this ghostly tale based on actual events. It's 1971 and Bud and his family move into an old house in Northern Arkansas. Bud soon discovers they live not far from a very interesting cave as well as a historic Civil War battle site. As odd things start to happen, Bud tries to solve the mysteries. But soon the entire family experiences a haunting situation.

If you enjoy ghost tales based on true events, then you'll enjoy Ghosts of Company K. This heartwarming story brings the reader into the life and experiences of a young boy growing up in the early 1970s. Seen through innocent and unsuspecting eyes, Ghosts of Company K reveals a haunting tale from the often unseen perspective of a young boy.

Oliver Phipps

BANE OF THE INNOCENT

http://www.amazon.com/dp/B00KWK7E1Q

"There's no reason for them to shoot us; we ain't anyone" - Sammy, Bane of the Innocent.

Two young boys become unlikely companions during the fall of Atlanta. Sammy and Ben somehow find themselves, and each other, in the rapidly changing and chaotic environment of the war-torn Georgia City.

As the siege ends and the fall begins in late August and early September of 1864 the Confederate troops begin to move out, and Union forces cautiously move into the city. Ben and Sammy simply struggle to survive, but in the process, they develop a friendship that will prove more important than either one could imagine.

Made in the USA
Lexington, KY
09 September 2017